GET REAL #1

Girl Reporter Blows Lid off Town!

Created by
LINDA ELLERBEE

AVON BOOKS NEW YORK

A Division of HarperCollinsPublishers

My deepest thanks to Katherine D
Anne-Marie Cunniffe, Lori Seidner, Whitney Ma
Roz Noonan, Alix Reid and Susan Katz, without whom
this series of books would not exist. I also want to thank
Christopher Hart, whose book, *Drawing on the Funny Side
of the Brain*, retaught me how to cartoon. At age 11,
I was better at it than I am now. Honest.

Drawings by Linda Ellerbee

AVON BOOKS TRADEMARK REG. U.S. PAT. OFF.
AND IN OTHER COUNTRIES, MARCA REGISTRADA, HECHO EN U.S.A.

Library of Congress Cataloging-in-Publication Data
Ellerbee, Linda.
    Girl reporter blows lid off town! / created by Linda Ellerbee.
        p.   cm. — (Get real ; #1)
    Summary: Casey Smith, an intrepid eleven-year-old journalist, revives
her middle school's defunct newspaper and investigates what looks like
an environmental pollution cover-up at the local paper mill.
    ISBN 0-06-440755-1 (pbk.) — ISBN 0-06-028245-2 (lib. bdg.)
    [1. Journalism—Fiction.   2. Newspapers—Fiction.   3. Schools—Fiction.
4. Pollution—Fiction.]   I. Title.   II. Series: Ellerbee, Linda.   Get real ; #1.
PZ7.E42845Gh   1999   99-23451
[Fic]—dc21   CIP
                                                                                        AC

Typography by Carla Weise
4   5   6   7   8   9   10
❖
First Edition

For the kids,
who always get real

Journalist Trapped in Body of Eleven-Year-Old Girl!

DRAMA CLUB MEETING
Wednesday at 3 P.M.

YEARBOOK
Help us make this year's edition special!

YOU'LL GET A "KICK" OUT OF SOCCER INTRAMURALS!

MY NAME IS Casey Smith and I am way too much for middle school.

But there I was.

Hugging my notebook, I scanned the flyers plastered on the bulletin board. The hall of Trumbull Middle School smelled of floor wax and shampoo.

1

And sweat.

Everyone was sweating out first-day jitters.

Myself included. Hadn't I agonized over choosing a shirt? T-shirt . . . or T-shirt? Baggy or baggy? And my jeans—faded blue or dark blue? Okay, that took about ten seconds.

I don't usually sweat fashion statements, even on the first day of school. And I don't waste time fussing with my brown hair. I also have brown eyes and pale skin that freckles and never tans. *Brown* freckles. What can you do when brown is your overall theme?

I do have one extraordinary feature. My ears. My elegant, shell-pink ears are perfect. (And I say that with total modesty, of course.) Otherwise, I'm small, but as my mother says, I have the energy and snap of a rubber band.

And at the moment I was ready to snap over the first day at middle school. Today was the official beginning of my career as a journalist. Sure, I'd kept a journal since I was a little kid. And I'd been published . . . sort of. In grade school I'd made copies of news stories I'd written and handed them out to everyone I knew.

Ten or eleven people.

What can I say? I was trapped in a pretty but painfully quiet town in the Berkshire Mountains of western Massachusetts.

"Trapped" being the operative word.

But there was hope. Here at Trumbull I could join the staff of a real newspaper. I could finally prove myself as a journalist. See, for me, it's not just the glory. Journalism *counts*. News is basically the answer to the question: What happened? If you don't know what happened, how do you know what to think?

Besides, I like secrets. That is, I like finding out other people's secrets. That's why I'm a reporter, not a photographer. Photographers don't get to ask questions. And reporters don't have to answer them. I like that part, too. Okay, maybe inside I'm a little shy, but don't tell anyone. Not that they'd believe you, anyway.

I hitched my backpack onto my shoulder. My notebook was fat with stories I'd drafted over the summer. The other reporters were going to be so happy to see me. So relieved I'd done my homework.

But . . . where *were* they? I'd been looking all day. Snooping between classes. Wandering the school at lunch during a very uneventful first day at Trumbull.

Do I sound bored out of my eyeballs? That's me, Casey Smith, restless, inquisitive and easily bored.

And it's easy to be bored at school. Just look

around. Lots of kids have that look. That "Oh, pullleeeze, not another fact about Thomas Edison!" expression. No wonder locker doors were slamming and kids were shuffling down the halls around me. Bored, bored, bored.

Again I stared up at the bulletin board.

```
• Get on-line with the MICROCHIPS! •
Computer Club meeting every Tuesday, 8 A.M.,
        bring your own floppies.
```

```
•      THREE CHEERS FOR TRUMBULL!      •
Cheerleading tryouts will begin in
two weeks. Two positions available.
Sign up with Ms. Tickner.
```

I scanned every single piece of paper. Twice. Then I folded my arms. "I don't believe this," I said under my breath. "It's not here!"

"Pretty shocking," a boy spoke up next to me.

Turning, I saw a kid about my height. He wore a loose denim shirt over a tie-dyed T-shirt, jeans and sandals with red socks. His shaggy brown hair was long enough to tuck behind his ears.

"You're looking for something about the paper, too?" I asked him.

"Me?" His gray eyes looked confused. "No, but paper definitely gets recycled."

4

Was this guy for real? "I meant the *school* newspa— Never mind. What were *you* looking for?"

"Frisbee club. Ultimate," he said. "They had three clubs in Oregon. At my old school."

"Oh." No wonder he seemed so spacey. He'd just moved here. "So . . . you're new?"

He nodded. "Yeah. Unless you believe in re-incarnation," he said. "I guess it's possible I was here in a previous life."

I wondered if this guy had been beamed here from another *planet*, not another life. But he had nice eyes and a genuine smile. Goofy, but genuine.

"Well . . . my name's Casey," I told him.

"I'm Ringo."

"Ringo? You mean like the   "

Brrring!

It was the bell for the next class—English. At last—the paper. Surely my English teacher would know about the school newspaper. "Well, see you around," I said.

"Yeah, a round," he said. "Like a Frisbee. Which is awesome, because I'm off to geometry."

"Watch out for the Bermuda Triangle."

"Definitely," he promised, shuffling down the hall.

Walking with purpose, I wove through the clustered students in the hall and found my

English class. A dozen kids had already settled into desks. Some faces were familiar from Abbington Elementary.

But there was one important face missing.

Griffin.

He was my best friend through elementary school. Now that he'd moved away, I was on my own. Weird. I was used to having him around. If he were here, he'd be leaning over, writing something like: "Forecast: Look out for a deadly dull day, with a chance of homework" in my notebook. He was also a writer.

I dropped into a chair beside the Kelleher twins, who I knew from grade school. They'd be fine about me sitting with them. The K-twins have no opinion, positive or negative.

"Hi, Casey," one girl said.

"Hi, Casey," the other echoed.

"Hey . . . girls." I stared, comparing features. I gave up. It was impossible to tell them apart. "Don't you ever feel like doing something radical? Like dressing in clothes that *don't* match?"

They both squinted at me.

"No way," one girl said. "Then we might not look so good together. We might, you know—"

"Clash," the other Kelleher twin finished.

So much for interesting conversation.

Cracking open my journal, I scrawled:

Griffin—come back!

I drew a line in my journal and added:

NOTE TO SELF: Story on twins who communicate without words? Telepathic? Or sci-fi story about twins who hate each other but share the same brain! Give idea to Griffin?

There was no teacherly person in sight. Would he or she make an announcement about the newspaper? Maybe that's how they handled it at Trumbull.

Well, no reason to waste time. Rubbing my palms on my jeans, I leaned back in my desk to observe—and write. All of the elementary schools around Abbington feed into Trumbull. There were kids from my grammar school in this class, as well from two other grade schools. I started a new page in my journal:

DATELINE: The First Thursday in September
Day One at Trumbull Middle School

STUDENT PROFILES: (FAMILIAR FACES)
BRANDON HABER— busted for
throwing rocks in third grade.
THE KELLEHER TWINS—matching
flowered shirts and blond ponytails. Can
anyone tell them apart? Does anyone
care?
ZACK AVERY—what color is his hair this
week?

Just then the bell rang and a heavyset man lumbered into the classroom. "I'm Mr. Baxter," he said. "And this is sixth-grade English. If that doesn't sound right to you, check your schedule and head out now," he added, grabbing an eraser with one beefy hand.

Beefy is a good overall word for Mr. Baxter. His face is square and reddish. He's got the build of a football player who escaped from training camp *before* calisthenics. But he's always moving. Fast.

He breezed through the class specs and got right to business, handing out books. A novel by Jane Austen.

I grinned. This guy didn't waste time. My kind

of person. The only problem? He was so wrapped up in talking about this author that I couldn't get a question in about the newspaper.

I was still jotting down notes about the author's life in my notebook when the bell rang. At last, I could find out about the newspaper. I finished the sentence. I looked up.

He was gone.

"Mr. Baxter!" I ran out after him.

"Tests and quizzes make up sixty percent of your grade," he said, never breaking stride. "Class participation counts for the rest."

"It's not about grades." I had to jog to keep up with him. "I want to find out about the school paper."

Mr. Baxter frowned at me. "You mean *Real News*?"

"Where can I sign up?" I had to walk double-time to keep up with him. "Did you know there isn't even a notice on the—"

"You can't sign up for *Real News*, Miss . . ."

"Casey Smith." I jogged ahead so that I could see his face. "What do you mean? The paper can't have a full staff. On the first day of school?"

"It has nothing to do with the staff." Mr. Baxter's brows knitted as he strode on. "You can't sign up . . . because the newspaper doesn't exist."

"Huh?"

Okay, it wasn't the most articulate response in the world. But even journalists have their off moments.

"I don't get it," I said, following him into the administration office. "If the paper doesn't exist, why does it have a name? It's even listed in the brochure that goes out to all the new students."

Mr. Baxter scanned the huge row of mailboxes as he talked. "*Real News* was the name of the school paper we had here years ago. The students stopped publishing it sometime back in the '80s."

"Why? Was there a scandal?" I tried to imagine the crisis that had shut down the paper. Had someone lied about a story? Forgotten to verify sources? Maybe there'd been a lawsuit.

He shook his head. "People got lazy. Too busy wondering when the next Kool and the Gang album would be released." He chuckled. I didn't see the humor.

"Are you trying to tell me Trumbull Middle School has *no* newspaper at all?" I asked. "Because the students are too *lazy*?"

"Sad, but true," Mr. Baxter said, nodding.

I felt my stomach bottom out.

No newspaper?

He might as well have said there was no oxygen. No water. No pizza. No takeout.

As Mr. Baxter headed out of the office, one teeny tiny little thought kept running through my head.

My life is over.

Journalists Sweat Issues at Writers' Boot Camp

To: Wordpainter
From: Thebeast
RE: First Fumble at Trumble

You sat with the Kellehers? No way! Those two make me nervous. Ever notice how they finish each other's sentences? Stay away from them—promise?

WHEN I READ Griffin's e-mail that night, I laughed. Too bad he was a gazillion miles away. Miles away but the only one around.

I squeezcd my perfect earlobes and groaned.

I was alone in my bedroom, stewing in my own juices. Notice how Griffin didn't mention the school paper? Probably didn't know what to say after I dumped my disappointment on him.

Everything was crashing down around me. No newspaper. No Griffin. No noise at home to distract me. Before I get into a funk, let me explain my idea of "home," which is probably more fast and free than yours.

My parents are working in Southeast Asia. They're part of a program called Doctors Without Borders. That means they travel around the world to places where doctors are needed.

This time it's the site of a chemical spill. There was an explosion at this factory, and toxic chemicals leaked into the groundwater, making lots of people sick.

So last month Mom and Dad headed off. They took my sixteen-year-old brother, Billy, along for the "cultural experience." Which is a nice way of saying they were afraid he would flunk high school if they left him here. Billy hates school.

Sometimes I miss my mom and dad. Sometimes I even miss Billy. But they're always just an e-mail away. And in some ways I think I got the best setup of this whole deal.

I got Gram.

Most people would picture a pudgy marshmallow lady who smells like perfume and bakes cookies.

Not my grandmother.

Gram is a journalist. You've probably seen her

on TV. Or maybe you've read one of her books. Gram has won some awesome awards. Even a Pulitzer Prize. Can you believe it?

When my parents headed off to Asia, Gram came to live with me. I couldn't believe she'd actually choose to leave New York City for Abbington. But Gram says she needed a little seclusion to work on a new book. And while there's not much going on in this little town in western Massachusetts, seclusion is one thing Abbington can offer.

Total seclusion. Total boredom.

The new book? Gram's experiences on Capitol Hill. That's Gram. She's always got something to say about everything, especially issues. Whether it's U.S. policy on China or the "issue" of who put the empty milk container back in the fridge.

Ever since she left her Manhattan townhouse to move in with me, home has been like boot camp for writers.

I love it.

Gram says that journalism is more than a bunch of talking heads and silly headlines. "It's simple," she says. "News is the answer to the question 'What happened?' The journalist is the one who finds out that answer."

I knew Gram would conjure a plan of attack for the situation at Trumbull. But she was locked in her office, frantically rewriting a chapter on some crooked politician.

I pushed away from my computer and kicked off my red hightops. They landed near a pile of a dozen or so Converse hightops in all different colors—my personal fashion statement.

My room is full of stuff my parents have brought back from places where they've worked. Shadow puppets from Indonesia. A chunk of concrete from the Berlin Wall. My bedspread was woven in a mountain village in Peru. And it's covered with silk pillows from China.

Best of all, though, my room is comfortable.

Sometimes I like to pretend it's the press room. The command center. The dusty old stuffed animals on that high shelf over the window are a pack of journalists. Each pane of the window is a TV monitor, showing news events all over the world.

I pulled a flashlight from a plastic storage bin on the floor and held it to my mouth—an impromptu microphone. Then I faced the camera—a penny jar, turned sideways on my desk.

"This is Casey Smith reporting from Trumbull Middle School. A school in crisis. A time of uncertainty. Student unrest. The threat of censorship hovers menacingly. The First Amendment to the Constitution is in grave danger. There is no school newspaper, which . . . which . . ."

I stumbled.

"Which is just so unfair. Because I'm ready to go. I've got stories that are ready to be published. I've got leads to investigate. And now what? I'm supposed to wait until high school?"

"Casey?" It was my grandmother.

A little embarrassed, I tossed the flashlight onto my desk and spun toward the door.

A knock, then Gram poked her head in. "I decided to come up for air." She sat on my bed and crossed her legs. "How was school?"

"Horrible."

Gram blinked. "That good?"

I spilled it all—no newspaper.

"Bummer." Gram frowned sympathetically.

"Bottom line?" I went on. "There is nothing for me at Trumbull Middle School. Absolutely no reason to grab my backpack and march off to that building tomorrow morning. Without a newspaper, school is just a bunch of classes."

"True." Gram nodded. She doesn't waste words. "What's your plan?"

"I don't know," I muttered. The bulletin board beside my desk is covered with news clippings and old stories and photos of my parents. I unpinned a story I'd written in third grade when our teacher, Ms. Lacey, organized a class play for Christmas.

~~The~~ ~~show~~ ~~is~~ st~~up~~id. It might be a good show. But that doesn't matter. Because it is not a <u>fair</u> show. MS. Lacey did not let students ~~audition~~ try out for parts. Instead, she picked her favorites to play the best roles. And that ~~stinks like~~ is not fair.

Okay, maybe the fact that I'd been forced to play an ear of corn *had* influenced my reporting. But, as Gram says, objectivity is impossible. You can't avoid bringing your own thoughts and experiences into your writing. It's better to try to be fair than objective.

"I've gotten better," I said suddenly.

"I should hope so," Gram said, putting my third-grade story on the desk. "Still, it's a good piece. I like all the things you self-published."

"But that was grade school," I said. "I have to move on, Gram. To a real newspaper."

"You're right. Absolutely." She stood up and raked her hair behind her ears. Gram has soft, short hair streaked with gold and silver and red. Low maintenance, she says. I think it looks nice.

"You need a newspaper," Gram said. "And I need to check a few facts in my latest chapter." She kissed my forehead, then headed out. "We'll figure it out in the morning. Now get some sleep. Let it stew."

Gram was big on letting things cook in your brain while you slept. The only problem was, after I slid between the flannel sheets, I couldn't sleep.

I felt mad. Disappointed. I wasn't going to take this without a fight.

If I had to, I'd put together a school newspaper myself.

That was it! Why hadn't I thought of it before? I shot up in bed as scenes flashed through my head. . . .

Surrounded by a team of eager journalists, Casey Smith barks out assignments.

Pencil in hand, Smith marks up copy and gives advice on rewrites.

And as the entire student body holds its collective breath, Smith leaps to her feet during an assembly and shoots a burning question at the principal.

It was time to haul *Real News* out of the closet.

The next morning, I got to school early and ran straight to Mr. Baxter's classroom. He was sorting books on the shelves by the window. He was doing it the way he seems to do everything— fast—as if he had somewhere important to go.

"Mr. . . . Baxter!" I gasped. I don't normally run.

"Casey, right? You're early for class." He checked his watch. "About . . . *four hours* early."

I slammed my books onto a desk. "I was thinking about the school paper."

"*Real News*?" Mr. Baxter grinned, then went back to lining up books. "Actually, I was talking to someone yesterday and—"

"I've got a great idea," I interrupted. When I get excited about something, I can't hold back. "*I am going to bring the paper back to life.*"

Mr. Baxter stood up and dusted off his hands. "Casey, you must have read my mind."

"I did?" This was going even better than I'd expected.

"As soon as Megan suggested it yesterday, I made an appointment to talk to Principal Nachman."

"Megan?" I blurted, following him to his desk. "Hold on a second. *I'm* the one who came up with the idea. Who's this Megan?"

"Megan O'Connor—another sixth grader. Very talented," Mr. Baxter explained. He began to collate and staple a stack of papers. "She won an award for a story she wrote at Millridge Elementary."

"Yeah, well . . ." I hadn't run all the way to school to hear Mr. Baxter sing the praises of some other kid. Especially one named Megan.

Her friends probably called her Muffy. "About the paper . . .?"

"Megan snagged me in the parking lot yesterday," Mr. Baxter said, stapling on. A virtual collating machine. "When she heard *Real News* was defunct, she asked me about starting up the paper again. Talked me into being faculty advisor." He smiled. "She'll be glad you're here to help."

"Um, *helper* isn't exactly the position I had in mind," I said, frowning. So much for letting things cook overnight. The editor job was slipping through my fingers.

"Well, we can figure out the specifics later," Mr. Baxter said. "First we have to get the okay for equipment and supplies. And an office. I wonder if anyone's using that closet beside the boiler room?"

Closet? Boiler room? Not exactly the office of my dreams.

"I'm meeting with Principal Nachman at lunch," he added, dropping the stapler into a drawer. "Why don't you and Megan come back here after school, and we can talk about how to get the ball rolling?"

"Sounds good," I told him.

Okay, it was a lame response. But I was caught off guard. I hate it when that happens.

I guess I should have been happy. At least there was going to *be* a school paper.

It was just that, well . . . I had started to think of *Real News* as *my* newspaper.

Get a grip, I ordered myself. If this Megan person was so *talented*, so driven that she thought of this idea before even *I* did, working on the paper with her would be great.

Yeah, right.

Reporter Mud Wrestles Sugarplum Fairy

MEGAN O'CONNOR.

I couldn't get that name out of my head as I passed the glass brick wall and joined the cafeteria line. Light glimmered off the pearly finish of the wall tiles. Rumor had it this room had gotten a face-lift over the summer. Hard to believe.

Megan O'Connor.

She was trying to steal away everything that mattered to me. And I couldn't let that happen.

GIRLS FACE OFF OVER WHO WILL BE EDITOR!

The headlines flashed in my brain as I shuffled through the cafeteria lunch line.

SMITH MUD WRESTLES O'CONNOR INTO GIANT MUD PIE!

That made me grin as I plunked a wrapped veggie burger on my tray.

"Are you actually going to *eat* that thing?" said someone next to me.

Glancing up, I recognized him. Dark hair, dark eyes, and a smile that would melt chocolate.

"You're Tyler McKenzie, right?" I asked, my voice squeaking a little. Last year, Tyler had been in the class across the hall. "I'm Casey."

"Right." Tyler had gotten a lot cuter over the summer. A lot cuter. His brown eyes were amazing. How had I missed that before?

"So, Casey, did you know there's no beef in that burger?"

Gingerly I opened the foil wrap and stared at the disk on a roll. The burger looked like a giant oatmeal cookie. Minus the sugar. Minus the fun. The swamp-thing burger.

"I figure it's safer than an E-coli burger," I said.

"True." Tyler smiled. "And no one's sure what's in these nuggets," he said, nodding at his tray.

"Mystery nuggets. What they do, I think, is fry up old erasers."

Tyler laughed, and I let myself smile. I noticed he was with some other boys. I also noticed that when they went to find a table, Tyler hung behind.

I couldn't believe it. He actually wanted to talk to me! Not that I care about stuff like that.

Okay, I care. But just a little.

"So, what do you think of—" I began.

"Hey!" Someone behind me interrupted. "Did you ever find out about the paper recycling program?"

Even before I looked, I knew who it was. "Hey, Ringo," I said, turning around. "It was the school *news*paper, and I'm checking it out. But I was talking to—"

"Coolness." Ringo held up a sandwich and a carton of juice. "The cafeteria is an amazing place, right? Kind of like the world, only smaller. And smellier. You could write an editorial."

"Good idea," I said, turning back to Tyler. But he was already heading toward the tables with his tray. Gone.

Talk about bad timing.

Ringo and I found a table beside the salad bar. A little too close to all those veggies to suit me, but the room was getting crowded. Before we attacked our food, we both pulled out notebooks and pens.

Was Ringo a reporter, too? Maybe the space cadet thing was a cover? Sipping my chocolate milk, I studied him. He was doodling around the edges of a page. A page of notes in a red notebook.

There's something fishy here. I wrote in my journal. *And it's not just the fish sticks!*

Finally, I had to ask him, "Ringo, are you a writer?"

His hand kept moving as he glanced up. "Sure, I can write. I mean, my parents insisted on it. The alphabet, and phonics. The whole deal."

"I'm not talking about first grade." I leaned across the table to check out the page.

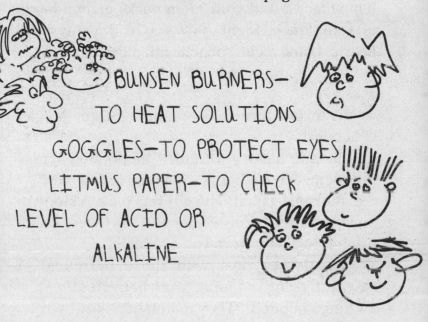

BUNSEN BURNERS—
TO HEAT SOLUTIONS
GOGGLES—TO PROTECT EYES
LITMUS PAPER—TO CHECK
LEVEL OF ACID OR
ALKALINE

Not story notes. It was science stuff surrounded by circles. Doodles of faces.

"Did you write down *everything* the teacher said?" I asked. Apparently he liked science.

He shrugged. "I like to keep my hands busy."

No kidding. While Ringo drew doodles on his doodles, I returned to my new target.

Megan O'Connor.

I studied the girls in the lunchroom. Was she here now? Or off in class?

"Megan O'Connor . . ." I muttered under my breath. "You're probably one of those girls who puts stickers on her books. Stickers with little happy faces. And your mom packs gummi bears in your lunch. Right now you're drawing little hearts. Using a cute pencil with a tassel on top."

"You doing someone's horoscope?" Ringo asked.

"Tracking down a subject. One Megan O'Connor."

"She's in history with me." He pointed across the room. "That's her . . . with the blond hair."

I looked. I gaped. The girl was pink. A study in pinkness. Okay, her sweater and skirt were a simple cut. But they were so . . . pink.

"What's the deal with those barrettes?" I asked, thinking out loud. "*Pink* barrettes?"

Ringo nodded. "They match her skirt."

I squinted. "What kind of reporter wears pink? Pink is not a serious color. I mean, pink is okay for cheerleaders. Maybe even the yearbook. But the school paper?"

"Maybe it's time for people to open up to pink," Ringo said with a shrug. "It might make the world a happier place, you know? We could have a slogan. Something like, 'Make pink, not war.'"

I snorted, and Ringo seemed surprised. The guy was actually serious. Go figure.

Across the room Megan was getting up to stack her tray.

Time to make my move.

I caught up to her at the trash and recycling bins. "Hi. You're Megan, aren't you?" When she seemed surprised, I added, "I'm Casey."

"Right. Mr. Baxter told me about you." A smile lit Megan's face. "I'm really glad you want to help get the school paper started again."

I glared at her. Why was everyone so hung up on this *helping* business?

When I didn't respond, she went on, "I think it's going to be a lot of fun!" She smiled again. Boy, was she ever perky.

"Fun?" I said grimly. "News is not *fun*, Megan. We're talking long hours and deadlines and digging beneath the surface to get the real story. It's about important issues. Gun control. Drug abuse. Racism. Pollution . . ."

Megan bit her lip. "Here? I doubt it."

Maybe Megan was popular, but she was clearly

out of touch with reality. "Those things can happen anywhere," I told her.

"Well, yeah." She brushed a strand of blond hair from her forehead. "We'll cover mostly school events, though. Sports and school dances and stuff."

I winced. This wouldn't be a newspaper. It would be a Hallmark card. "Sports and dances?"

She nodded. "Sure."

"Why don't we just publish the list of kids who made the cheerleading squad?" I asked sarcastically. "And birthday greetings for all the teachers."

"What a sweet idea," Megan gushed, her eyes sparkling with warmth.

Megan seemed nice enough, in a candy-coated way. Sort of dipped in goo. The kind of person who does good deeds. Probably has a SAVE THE WHALES sticker on her bedroom wall, but only if it doesn't clash with her wallpaper, which would be flowered, of course. Little bitty *pink* flowers, I'll bet. What she didn't have was the hard-hitting edge a journalist needs.

"Look," I said, "are you sure that working on a school paper is for you? Wouldn't you be happier in drama club? Or on the cheerleading squad? Or—"

"I plan on trying lots of different activities.

Including the newspaper," Megan interrupted.

"Or . . . or the yearbook committee," I went on. "People like you are perfect for Yearbook."

"What's *that* supposed to mean?" Megan frowned. For the first time she looked annoyed. "Look, I don't want to fight about this. Mr. Baxter said I could get *Real News* going again, and that's what I'm going to do. Do you want to help or not?"

"I'm not going to *help*," I said, gritting my teeth. "I am going to be the editor."

It was out. War had been declared.

"Oh, really?" Megan crossed her arms. All of a sudden she didn't look like she was dipped in goo. *Steel* was more like it. "We'll see about that."

Okay, this was a game I could play. I crossed my arms, too. "Yes. We will."

Booby Traps Found at Power Center

WHEN MEGAN AND I got to Mr. Baxter's office after school, we each started bombarding him with our side of the story.

"Mr. Baxter," Megan began. "I get along with everyone. Just ask around. I like things to run smoothly, and—"

"There's no way I'm working for the Sugarplum Fairy," I said flatly. "I say we cut the—"

"Calm down!" Mr. Baxter threw up his hands.

He looked back and forth between us. "I get the picture. Unfortunately, we don't need *two* editors."

"I am definitely more qualified," I stated, glaring at Megan. "When there was no newspaper in grade school, I published my own. I've been working all summer. I—"

"But, Mr. Baxter," Megan said, frowning, "I thought you said—"

"I think the fairest solution is to let the staff decide," Mr. Baxter said quickly. "Once you have a crew assembled, you can all vote on it. But that's down the road. For the first edition you can edit each other. Share the load."

Megan nodded. "Right."

"Absolutely," I agreed quickly, not to be outdone. I pulled my folder out of my backpack. "That's why *I'm* here. I've got seven or eight stories that are ready to go."

Megan's mouth dropped open. "You . . . you've already written stories for the paper?"

"A writer writes." I handed the folder to Mr. Baxter. I wanted him to read my work and love it.

"Megan should read them first," he said.

"I'd be happy to take a look," she said.

"Good," said Mr. Baxter.

I swallowed hard as my stories disappeared into Megan's backpack.

"Now . . ." Mr. Baxter went on. "Ms. Nachman said we can use the old storage room by the theater. It's filled with typewriters. Dinosaurs. But the math department just got new computers, so maybe we can snag a few of their old ones. And an old printer."

"What about other supplies?" I asked.

"Right," Megan added. "We'll need paper and toner—"

"And tiny microphones and camcorders," I cut in.

"I'm afraid high-tech equipment is not in the budget, Casey," Mr. Baxter said, taking a paper out of his briefcase. "But here's our supply list. You can pick this stuff up from the main office."

"Great!" I said. "I'll go get it now." I grabbed at the list, but he held it back.

"Whoa! You girls can go together, okay? Just give me a second to double-check this thing."

As he scanned the list, I glanced at Megan, who was deflating like a balloon. *What is her problem?* I wondered as she checked her watch and frowned.

"Looks good." Mr. Baxter handed me the list. "The office secretary will let you sign the stuff out. Just do me a favor. Try not to mess up the supply room. Ms. Kiegel will fry me."

"Megan will wipe off our fingerprints," I said, motioning for her to follow.

"Umm, I can't go," she blurted out. "I have a . . ." She paused, as if the words were hard to say. "There's a yearbook meeting in three minutes."

"Yearbook?" I said quietly. I wanted to dance around and say, "I knew it! I knew it!" But for once

I held back. I had already written most of the issue. I could afford to be generous.

"Nothing says I can't do both!" Megan insisted.

"Of course not," Mr. Baxter agreed. "Go to your meeting. Casey can get the supplies and set up."

"But I'll work on the paper this weekend at home," Megan said. "We'll need more reporters. Photographers, too. I'll make a poster to recruit people."

The thought of Megan kneeling over a poster made me smile. While Megan sprinkled glitter, I would set up the power center.

"Have fun at Yearbook," I said, rolling up the list. "I'll phone in from the field." I headed for the door.

"Casey," Mr. Baxter called after me. "There's no budget for cellulars. . . ."

I just waved him off and tramped down the hall, my sneakers squeaking on the tiles. I was a reporter on assignment.

My mission: Set up the newsroom.

CHAPTER 5

Walls of Gray Paint Cause Writer's Block

DATELINE: Monday, A.M., Live from the newsroom

Two windows painted shut. Floor tiles missing chips at the corners. Four stodgy old desks, lined up like cows waiting to cross the road. And miles of tacky gray paint.

Welcome to the REAL NEWS control center.

I put down my journal, leaned out the door of the old storeroom and tried to suck in some of the good air from the hallway.

My new office was stuffy. And how was anyone supposed to think surrounded by all that shiny gray paint? It was probably destroying my brain cells.

It had taken awhile to find this closet on Friday afternoon. I had traipsed through an entire corridor of science labs with Bunsen burners and tall counters and stools and skeletons hanging beside the blackboards.

Then I'd gotten lost in another wing of classrooms with maps that covered the walls. Rows of computers. Dressing rooms behind the theater. Art studios with easels and skylights. All that stuff, and you'd think they'd give us a news center with more personality than an elephant's rear end.

Still, the place was shaping up. Over the weekend the janitor had cleared out most of the typewriters. I'd stocked the room with paper and pencils and all that stuff, but we wouldn't have computers until Mr. Baxter got the okay.

The air felt stale. The room was cold. Dead. Impersonal. I'd taped up a map of the world, planning to flag locations as we did stories. But even that got swallowed up in the gray gloom.

One major thing was missing: the noise made by a bullpen of reporters.

Of course, Megan probably had a few friends

she wanted to invite on to the staff. I squinted at the empty room and imagined an army of pink-and-white preppie Pop Tarts at the desks.

Scary.

It was clearly up to me to find real reporters. Kids who cared about the world beyond the doors of this school. Journalists with energy and drive . . . and the good sense to vote me in as editor.

No one came to mind.

I decided to let the problem percolate while I worked on other things. Cracking open my journal, I scanned the list of stories I'd given Megan.

News From the Hill (<u>Capitol</u> Hill)

Alfred Trumbull: Who Was He? Who Cares?

Beauty Pageants: Pretty? Says Who?

The Presidency: Let a Woman Do It.

Something Fishy: Is Our River Sick?

The Middle East: What Next?

There was also "Cleaning Green," a story about a bunch of kids who ran a local house-cleaning service over the summer. I liked it because they used only natural cleaners like baking soda and vinegar.

I ran my pencil down the list.

They were good stories. Solid. Important. Well written. But none of them were big enough. I mean *blow-the-lid-off-this-town* big!

Write BIG story! I jotted in the margin.

Megan stepped into the closet-office and smiled. Today she wore a blue jumper over shiny white leggings. Ralph Lauren meets the Jetsons.

"You started setting up? Good! Good job, Casey." It sounded like she was talking to a trained seal.

"Throw me a fish, and I'll clap my flippers," I said.

"Excuse me?" She squinted.

"You have no sense of humor," I told her.

"Sure I do." She sat down behind a desk with tic-tac-toe games etched into the surface. "What was the joke, anyway?"

"Forget it. Did you read my stories?"

"I read them." Megan pretended to be busy, opening and closing desk drawers. She probably was trying to avoid gushing over my stories. "And I made three posters over the weekend. For the lobby, the second floor and one for outside the gym."

"And . . ." I prodded. I didn't care about stupid posters. We had *real* work to do. "The stories?"

"They're well written."

For a moment I basked in the praise. Maybe there *was* some gray matter under that blond hair, after all. "I know we still need a front-page story," I said. "But otherwise, the paper is filled."

"Not exactly." The words echoed in an empty file drawer, where Megan was hiding her head.

I frowned. "Megan, come out and talk to me."

She straightened up reluctantly and turned to me.

"The thing is—" She paused to pull my folder of stories out of her pack. "I'm not sure any of your stories is right for *Real News*."

"What?" Forget what I said about gray matter.

"Okay, maybe with some work the one about Alfred Trumbull would be okay. But the other stories have nothing to do with the kids in this school. No relevance. Who cares about a beauty pageant in Chicago? Or that some scientists are studying the Sussex River? It doesn't even run near the school."

I couldn't believe what I was hearing. "But there are dead fish," I pointed out.

"In a river that doesn't even run near the school," Megan repeated.

"So you're saying it only matters if toxic water is squirting out of the drinking fountains in the school lobby? That we should only care about things that directly affect us?"

"No," she said, frowning.

I glared at her, folding my arms. She looked uncomfortable. I kept glaring.

"Not really. Well, sort of. All right, that's kind of what I'm saying. Look, Casey, we're two sixth graders at the bottom of the rung in middle school. How are we going to get anyone to read *Real News*? By publishing stories that interest them."

"Prom notes and bake sales?" My voice squeaked. It does that when I'm nervous.

"If we need to." She handed me the folder.

"No way!" I waved my stories at her. "You're wrong. Kids care about the world. They're not all obsessed with watching TV and hanging at the mall."

Megan shrugged. "We'll see. I set up a suggestion box in the lobby. We'll let the students decide what they want to read about."

A suggestion box. How elementary. As in *elementary school*. How typical of Megan. How . . .

Perfect. Yes, I could make Megan's grammar-school tactics work for me. I knew how to get kids thinking about news. There was a way to fill that box with suggestions and prove my point. Nothing dishonest, of course.

Nobody said we couldn't campaign a little.

"Okay," I told Megan. "It's a newspaper for kids. Let the kids decide."

"Great," she said, blinking with surprise at how quickly I'd agreed to her idea. If she had known me better, she would have realized I was up to something. She'd learn.

"We'll go through the box tomorrow after school."

I stood up and tucked my journal away. "Okay. But you'd better take a second look at my stuff." I hitched my backpack on my shoulder. "Because it's exactly what kids will want. I guarantee it."

I barreled out of the office and almost mowed down a girl on her way in.

"Well, knock me over, why don't you?" she snapped. "Some people need remedial work in the manners department. You know?"

I stepped back to check out the chick with attitude. She was Hispanic, with piercing brown eyes and reddish hair that spewed from her ponytail like a glittery fountain. She wore baggy jeans and a red shirt that didn't quite make it to her brown suede belt.

But looks aside, this girl had a certain drive. A push that would make her stand out in a crowd. Gram calls it boom-chicka-boom.

"Sorry," I said. "I didn't see you, and I'm in a huge hurry."

"Yeah, yeah, so am I. In fact," she said, turning to Megan.

As if I wasn't even there.

"Just take these." She flipped open her backpack and started digging around inside. "I don't have time for this school paper nonsense. But you can use some of these pictures I've already taken. You do what you got to do with the photos and give the rest back to me, okay?" She handed a manila envelope to Megan and headed out again.

"Wait," Megan said. The girl stopped. "This is Casey, the girl I told you about. Casey, meet Toni Velez, our staff photographer."

"Staff photographer . . ." I said slowly. So Megan was already picking staff without me?

"I don't think so." Toni rolled her eyes. "No way am I going to work on a newspaper. I do enough work for school. And I don't join clubs."

"It's *not* a club," I snapped. No way was I going to let anyone start calling journalism a warm-and-fuzzy club.

But Toni was already tramping down the corridor.

I turned to Megan. "So you decided that she's good enough to be on staff?"

Already halfway down the corridor, Toni wheeled around and called back, "Excuse me? Are you referring to me?"

"Check out her stuff," Megan said quietly. "She's really talented."

I pulled the photographs out of the envelope, knowing Toni was boomeranging back in attack mode.

One glance was enough. She *was* talented.

I bit my lip as I flipped through the photos. The shots were clear and focused. And there was something else. She had caught the world in motion. People's hands swinging. Feet dancing. Flags waving. Trucks rolling. Smiles fading, eyes shifting.

"Whoa," I said, sort of to myself.

"Excuse me?" Toni piped up. "Is that the best you can do? Because I heard that you're a writer, and if you are going to write for this paper, you are going to need a vocabulary."

"Your pictures belong in a paper," I said, looking her in the eye. "The way you catch things as they're happening? Your shots have action. *And* emotion. Just the sort of photos we need."

Her face relaxed into a look of satisfaction. "That's better. Okay, then. I'll come by when I have more stuff." And she traipsed off again.

"Wait," I called after her. "We have to work together on this. We'll need you to get some shots to go with our stories."

But Toni was gone, her heels echoing in the hall.

"She's a find, isn't she?" Megan beamed with pride.

"Oh, sure," I said, slapping the photos onto a desk. "We can make up stories to go with her photos. Who cares about the news? Who cares about the truth? Or justice! We'll just do . . . photo essays!"

"You're being sarcastic," Megan said defensively.

"Who, me?"

"Yes, you. And it's not very . . . nice."

Nice, cute, sweet—they were Jell-O words. Flabby. Jiggly. And they dissolved to nothing.

"Megan, we need a photographer we can work with. Someone who'll cooperate." I tried to say this patiently. At least I tried.

"So she has a strong personality," Megan said.

"Is that what you call it?" I responded. "Try *impatience. Or aggression.* Along with just a touch of *hostility.*"

Megan frowned. "So we'll talk to her. *I'll* talk to her. But take another look at her photos. See if there's anything in this batch that you can work with. Something might spark your interest."

With a pained look I picked up the stack and sifted through it again. One photo showed a dog yanking on his leash. "Let's see. We can run this with an editorial on leash laws," I said.

Megan looked over my shoulder. "I guess," she said tentatively.

"I'm *kidding*." Sheesh. No humor at all.

Another photo captured a row of flags, waving gently. Behind them were slivers of faces. Kids in a marching band. Proud. Happy. It was probably from the big Fourth of July Parade held in Abbington every year.

"We could use this. You could say something like: 'Stand up and cheer! *Real News* is back!'"

"That's great!" Megan said.

"Again—*kidding*."

She frowned. The girl did not get sarcasm.

I studied a shot of the Sussex River, which ran through part of Abbington. This shot showed a security fence zigzagging through bushes. A square, matchbox building sat up on the embankment.

"What's this?" I asked.

Megan glanced at it. "The paper mill. Every sixth-grade social studies class takes the tour. My class went Friday."

That rang a bell. My class was set to go Wednesday.

"What's the deal with these pipes?" I asked. Three round pipes spewed dark, sluggish liquid.

Megan shrugged. "You don't see that on the tour. That part of the mill is hidden by lots of weeds and bushes."

"Hmmm." My fingers tingled. I got that feeling

whenever I sensed a story. There was a mystery waiting to be solved in this photo. "A school trip definitely needs coverage in the paper."

"Wait a second." Megan eyed me cautiously. Finally she was getting wise to me. "What, exactly, are you saying?"

"That the mill might just be polluting the river, right under our noses."

Megan frowned. "You're guessing, right?"

"Hypothesizing," I corrected her. "I need to check it out. But wait."

I went to my folder and handed her the page with the headline "Pollution: Is Our River Sick?"

"Project Green is tracking toxins in the river," I said. "Actually, they're doing a study on the fish population. Which is not doing well."

"Dead fish and a paper mill?" Megan shook her head. "What's the connection, Casey?"

"This mill is dumping *something*. Maybe there's a link between the dumping and the dead fish."

"Casey," Megan said, holding up her hands. "Let's not go crazy with this."

I just smiled down at Toni's photo.

Crazy? No.

Aggressive? Yes.

CHAPTER
6

Would You Eat These Chemicals on Your Breakfast Cereal?

"So . . . THAT'S WHAT WE'RE DOING," I said, wiping my sweaty palms on my jeans. Could the kids tell that I was nervous? "Bringing *Real News* back to life. But we're determined to make it a paper *you* want to read."

I paced across the front of Mr. Baxter's classroom as I spoke.

The kids in my English class stared back. Their faces were different from up here. Did they always look so bored? So tired? So . . . blank?

From the back of the classroom, Mr. Baxter nodded, encouraging me. Or was he telling me to wrap it up?

Taking a deep breath, I continued. "We set up a suggestion box in the lobby. But, hey—who ever pays attention to that stuff?"

46

A few laughs.

Maybe I was reaching them.

"So I'm here to find out what you want to read about. What do *you* care about? Terrorism? Feeding the homeless? Megaviruses? Gun control? The migration of killer bees? What scares you? What's bugging you?"

"Too many English assignments," someone moaned.

"I heard that, Zack," Mr. Baxter grumbled from the back of the room. "So write it in the form of a proposal," he went on, lumbering up to the front of the room. How that man manages to lumber so quickly is one of the mysteries of the universe.

"I want each of you to write up one or two ideas," Mr. Baxter said. "When you're done, pass it over to me. I'll put them in the suggestion box. Then crack open the Austen novel."

Relief sank over me as I sat down. Good thing I'm a writer. Public speaking makes my eyeballs sweat.

As the students scrawled their suggestions, I hoped that I'd put them on the right track.

I would get twenty-two suggestions.

Twenty-two requests for global issues.

And not one mention of the Valentine's Day Dance.

Take that, Megan O'Connor!

After dinner that night I went to my room and turned on my computer. I needed information about paper manufacturing.

Time to go on-line.

Kicking a mound of my dirtiest dirty clothes into the corner, I plunked down into my desk chair. My parents have never been thrilled with the state of my room. Sometimes Mom e-mails me:

Love you, Casey. Don't read all night. And clean your room!

As if she can see me.

But a room can only be called messy if you can't find stuff. And I know exactly where everything in my room is. Most of the time.

I pushed back my collection of Tibetan river stones and opened my journal beside the keyboard. Then I turned on the computer, began punching keys and started surfing the 'net.

I found a page with a link to the mill's web site. Clicking on the link, I watched as the page started to paint on the screen.

There was a slick photograph of the mill. A square building overlooking a majestic river.

Clean and neat.

Toni had caught the same view of the mill in her photograph. But the web site photograph failed to include one important thing that Toni's photo had—

The image of three pipes spewing foul-looking liquid into the river.

"No surprise there," I murmured. If the company was polluting, why advertise it?

The web site gave some historical information. I found out Riverhead Paper was one of the oldest companies in town. There were statistics for how much paper the company produced. There were also more photos:

A truckload of lumber.

A giant log disappearing into a wood chipper.

A twisted line of tanks and pipes and metal towers.

A technician beside a roller that was bigger than a city bus.

All pristine. All by-the-book. Nothing I could really sink my teeth into.

Then I came across something that surprised me.

An environmental report. "Environmental Safety and Health Report."

In the report Riverhead Paper *admitted* that there was runoff from the mill. There was a pie chart that showed the breakdown of wastes:

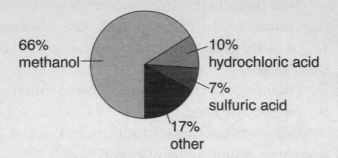

What *was* this stuff? It was like reading the wrapper of the nonfat cheese food my mom buys.

I sat there, staring at the pie chart. Toxic pie. Baking in the Sussex River.

The report went on to state that it was all okay. Riverhead Paper was "within acceptable limits." That runoff waste was perfectly legal.

Well, we'd see just how acceptable the waste was. I had a hunch from Toni's photograph that the whole story hadn't been told.

Time to knuckle under. I love following a lead.

I tapped into the on-line encyclopedia to learn how a paper mill operates.

I downloaded articles about the impact of paper manufacturing on the ecosystem.

I hit on a campaign for stronger government regulations of industry waste.

I searched environmental interest groups

until I found Project Green—the one studying the fish population of the Sussex River. They had found that the fish were not doing so well. But last time I checked, they hadn't found the cause of the epidemic. I was scrolling through the info when—

"Casey?"

My grandmother glowed red in the doorway. Gram has this red silk bathrobe with a colorful embroidered dragon. She got it while on assignment in Asia, and she wears it when she's relaxing. Today it was belted over sweats and a yellow T-shirt.

"I'm finished!" Gram said, clicking her fingers like a flamenco dancer. "Finito. Chapter e-mailed in." She twirled into my room. "What are you cooking up?"

"Toxic pie." I picked up a stack of paper from the printer and waved it at her. "Gram, do you have any idea what goes on inside a paper mill?"

"I have a feeling you're going to tell me." She stopped twirling. Gram is a good listener.

"Chemical pulp bleaching. That's when they use chlorine to make the paper white. Which happens to pollute! We're talking cancer-causing dioxins, chlorinated organic pollutants. Hydrochloric acid. Sulfuric acid. And that stuff is dumped right into the river!"

Gram's smile melted into a sad nod. "Welcome to the real world, Casey," she said. "It isn't always perfect."

"No kidding!" I said. "I mean, there's a lot of wildlife around the Sussex. Frogs and algae and birds and fish. And people *swim* in it!"

Gram sat down on the end of my bed.

I went on. "And what about the people who eat diseased fish from the river? Are they going to get sick? This is unbelievable! And do you know what the worst thing is? It's legal!"

I handed her a copy of the environmental report I had printed out. "They call it acceptable emissions. Legal limits. As if *any* level of pollution is all right!"

Gram skimmed the report. "Hydrochloric acid? I think they use that to pickle metal. And methanol . . . I need to brush up on my chemistry. But I definitely wouldn't want to cook spaghetti in a pot of this gobbledygook."

I clicked the mouse, and the web site for Riverhead Paper flashed on the screen again. "I *knew* it. I knew I was on to a major scoop."

"Hold up a sec," Gram said. "What's your story?"

"Riverhead Paper is polluting the Sussex," I answered. "That's news."

"Is it?" Gram challenged. "Can you prove that

the mill is polluting beyond legal limits?"

"No, but how could *any* amount be legal?" I countered. "A bucket of toxic waste is too much. Even an eyedropperful!"

"In a perfect world. But the law allows mills to dump *some* of their runoff. Not enough to do significant harm to the river. Or so we hope."

"Then it's a stupid law," I retorted.

"Your view would make a fine *editorial*," Gram said. "But you don't have the facts for a news story."

I shook my head firmly. Gram is an amazing person and an awesome reporter. But she was wrong about this. Way wrong. "This is big. Pollution, right down the block," I insisted. "You know how people are always saying to think globally and act locally? Well, I'm going to take action."

I spun my chair around and clicked the mouse. "I'm going to *make* this a story."

Cooties Found in Water Supply!

I HAVE NEVER been a morning person. And it didn't help that I'd stayed up late last night, surfing the 'net. So when I hit the newspaper office first thing Tuesday morning, I tried to control my grouchiness. I would go easy on Megan.

At least, I would try.

"I've got our front-page story," I said, handing her the crisp pages.

"Another story! You're so fast," she said. But her smile was cautious, and her voice was not as perky as usual. Like she was sizing up the enemy.

"'Is Chemical Waste Ever Safe?'" Megan read the headline.

"I hope you're not planning to read the whole thing out loud," I said.

"Sorry." As she started reading to herself, I tried to decide which desk I liked best. Not that there was much difference. All the desks had scarred tops and scratched drawers. The "distressed" look in furniture.

Suddenly Megan looked up and snapped her fingers. "How about a staff meeting after school?"

"Staff?" I repeated. "What staff?"

"You, me, and Toni. And anyone else who signs up. I can't believe no one else has signed up yet. What are we doing wrong?"

I chewed a pencil. "Could it be the smiley faces on the recruitment poster?"

She tucked a lock of perfect hair behind one ear. "Do you think so?"

"Please . . . read first. Then talk."

"Gotcha."

I tried to distract myself. I even went through a few desk drawers and cleaned out the old napkins and paper clips and tacks that had been left behind.

But I couldn't resist. I sneaked a peek at Megan. Did she like it? I couldn't tell. Her lips were pursed in concentration. Her shoulders back, posture erect.

At last, she glanced up. "I like this part." She pointed to a paragraph. I read it over her shoulder.

```
Check your watch. Got the time?
Because right now toxic chemicals
```

are pouring into the Sussex River.
Tick-tick. Polluting the water.
Tick. Killing plants. Tick-tick.
Flowing into the fish your dad
plans to bake for dinner. Tick.
Seeping into the groundwater under
your backyard.

"You like that?" I beamed. Megan might be smarter than I'd given her credit for. "I want kids to see how it affects them, personally. That Riverhead Paper has to be stopped. It's the perfect front-page story for our first issue."

"Actually . . ." Megan frowned as she hesitated. "What I meant was, I like your writing. You have a real way with words. But you're a little light on facts here. You don't prove that Riverhead Paper is doing anything illegal. They *are* dumping. But it's within legal limits. You say so yourself. We may not like the dumping, but the government allows it."

Gram's criticism, once again. And equally wrong.

"Okay, then," I snapped. "How about a little hydrochloric acid on *your* fish sticks?"

"But you say here that those are acceptable emissions. And you can't blast Riverhead just because *you* don't like what they're doing. Besides, a lot of kids' parents work there. My friend Heather's mother works in their accounting department. Tyler McKenzie's dad works there, too."

"Tyler McKenzie?" My face felt hot. "Really? Do you know him?"

Megan shrugged. "He's in my English class. But back to the mill. You'll get a better picture of things when your class takes the tour. You'll see some of the machines at work. When do you go?"

"Tomorrow."

"Good. You might change your mind when you see the place. It's impressive. It's clean. And face it. The world needs paper. *We* need paper to put out a news*paper*, Casey."

My fingers balled into fists. "So we should junk up the planet to get what we want?"

I knew I was being stubborn. But I couldn't stop myself. I had stayed up late to work on this story. No way would I give it up.

Megan smoothed the papers neatly. "This is a good editorial. You cut right to the bone. But to say Riverhead is doing something *wrong*—that's your opinion. Unless you back it up with facts."

I raked a hand through my hair. It was exactly what Gram had told me. But hearing it from Megan was more than I could take.

Suddenly I couldn't stand the sight of her pale pink blouse with its crisp cuffs neatly turned up.

Or the matching pink Swatch strapped around her wrist.

Little Miss Pink-and-Perfect know-it-all. Well, she wasn't a real reporter like me. No way. Just because the factory *looked* nice on the tour didn't mean it *was* nice. I had almost made the biggest mistake in journalism—I trusted what a company said about itself.

Who's to say Riverhead wasn't lying about its emissions? They sure didn't put any photo of pollution-dripping pipes on their web site.

I snatched my story and shoved it in my backpack. "You want facts? I'll get you facts."

I was halfway to the door when Megan called out, "Don't forget the meeting."

"Just hold the front page for me," I called, stomping out of the office.

Get the facts.

Hadn't I done that? I thought as I sat in Mr. Lanigan's class. I had already finished the math problems he'd put up on the board. Math has always been easy for me. It must be the logical way I think. I like dealing with concrete issues, like how long it takes a train traveling 150 miles an hour to reach a city 625 miles away.

GET THE FACTS!

I had just spent most of one night surfing the

web for facts. But what I needed wouldn't be found on a web site or in a book.

I needed firsthand information. I needed a person, someone on the inside to talk to. What I needed was a *source*.

But first I needed a plan. I took out my journal.

* Call Project Green for a copy of its study of fish in Sussex. Can PG link sick fish to Riverhead Paper???

* Verify legal limits of toxic chemicals. Find out if Riverhead Paper is telling the truth—does it REALLY obey legal limits???

During lunch I camped out at the pay phones off the school lobby. I had money enough for two short, local phone calls.

First target—Project Green.

Its web site had mentioned the study on the Sussex River, but the results weren't posted.

The guy who answered explained that the study was ongoing. "I'm really not the person to talk to," he told me. "You need Dawn Forrest. Dr. Dawn, we call her. Is there a number where you can be reached?"

I gave him my home phone number and dialed my second target—Riverhead Paper. That got me to the company's voice mail. Afraid of falling into an electronic abyss, I pressed two for Public Relations and got someone named Ms. Dombrowski.

"This is Casey Smith," I said forcefully, "a journalist for *Real News*."

"A journalist?" She paused. "I'm sorry, what's the name of your paper?"

"Real News."

"And where is it published?" she asked.

"Right here in Abbington."

"Really? I've never seen it, I don't think."

The bell was going to ring. I didn't have time to give her the history of *Real News*. And I didn't think she'd be too impressed to learn it was a school paper.

I pressed on. "I'm calling to arrange an interview with the president of the company about chemical emissions the plant is pouring into the river."

"Really?" Did she sound slightly alarmed? Go, Casey! "What was your name again?"

I told her, and she made me spell it out. But how many ways can you spell "Smith?" Ms. Dombrowski was definitely the slow, methodical type.

"Okay, Miss Smith," she said. "The president of the company works out of our corporate headquarters in Chicago. And to be honest, he doesn't have much time to meet with reporters. But I'd be happy to send you a brochure."

"Save the paper. I've checked your web site." I bit my lower lip. "Isn't there anyone at the plant that I can meet with?"

The bell rang for class, and I couldn't hear her at all. When the noise stopped, I had a bad feeling about what was coming next.

"Of course, Casey. You can meet me," Ms. Dombrowski said reassuringly. The bell blew my cover. She knew I was a kid. Otherwise she would not have called me Casey. "Let's see . . . I'm booked for the next few weeks. School tours. But after that—"

Frustrated, I glanced at my notes as she cheerfully babbled on, probably relieved.

I wouldn't get what I needed from Ms. Dombrowski. We weren't on the same side here. And no way would she take a kid seriously. Gripping my pen, I scrawled in my journal:

Get _inside_ source at Riverhead!!!

And I had the perfect connection. Someone who had personal access to an inside source. Someone who was related to a factory worker. Someone who was in the same building with me right this minute.

Now I only had to drum up the nerve to talk to Tyler McKenzie.

Poem Trounced by Big Sneakers and Bigger Ego

Tyler McKenzie.

I glanced up to see if the other girls in the locker room were watching.

No. There was only a handful of stragglers, slamming doors and tying sneakers. Most of the girls had already headed out to play basketball or field hockey or some other uncivilized form of torture with a ball.

I sat alone on a bench with my journal. Not that I was going to try to dodge gym today. Yesterday I'd noticed that Tyler had phys ed at the same time I did. He was probably outside right now, sprinting on the track or dribbling a basketball through traffic cones.

This was the perfect chance to snag him. So why was I so nervous? Why hadn't I actually gotten off the bench and gone outside?

Tyler McKenzie.

I'm not one of those girls who writes the name of the boy they like over and over again. Then they add little hearts. And rainbows. And flowers. Then they add their first name to his last one. Give me a break.

Tyler was a source. And that's why his name was in my journal. The only reason. I'm a journalist looking for a source, not a boyfriend. End of story.

Casey Smith McKenzie.

Well, it didn't look bad, I had to admit.

"You're one of mine, aren't you?"

I slammed my journal shut and looked into the hazel eyes of my gym teacher, Ms. Tickner. She was a petite woman with short blond hair, an upturned nose and *huge* eyes. Right now they were staring at me.

"I'm on my way, Ms. Tickner," I promised. I stood up and shoved my journal into my locker. "I'm not really up for a game today, but I'll definitely hit the field." There was no game on the face of this earth that I was ever up for.

"You gotta play to win," she said in a squeaky voice.

I was beginning to see why kids called her Tinker Bell.

"You know, Ms. Tickner, sports and I—we aren't on the same page. In fact, every other girl out there is better off if I stay away from the field. Far away."

Her hazel eyes flashed with the challenge I presented. I could see her thinking, How long will it take to make this girl a lean, mean athletic machine?

"What's your name?" was all she said.

"Casey Smith."

"Okay, Casey." She pointed to the door. "Let's go. Double-time now."

Tinker Bell escorted me out the door to the field, making me jog all the way. The other girls huddled around her as she squeaked out basketball tips. Did I care that you were only supposed to bounce the ball with one hand at a time? What was the point?

Did I mention that I hate gym?

I checked the other athletic fields. Silhouettes of kids and balls bobbed over the horizon. It was warm and sunny. A perfect day to skip gym. But I had a mission. Find Tyler.

Another class was already on one field, scampering over dirt clods. Hockey sticks hacked through the air. The Kelleher twins grinned identically as they pummeled the ground with sticks.

Behind the backstop a boy swung the bat and bolted down the field. The other guys yelled something at him. "Run! Slide! Keep low!"

As if they could save the stupid baseball game by yelling.

Did I mention that I'm not crazy about sports?

Then I spotted Tyler off to the side of the baseball field, watching the game.

This was it. My chance to talk with Tyler *and* bug out of the battle of the balls. But could I escape Tinker Bell?

I hung back as everyone counted off for teams. Fortunately, there were too many girls for two teams and not enough for four teams. I would have to wait for the next round. Darn it.

I moved toward the baseball field. I knew I wasn't supposed to leave the area. But this was just a trip to a neighboring field. Lucky for me Ms. Tickner was too busy squeaking about "double dribbling" to notice that one of her students was slinking away.

By the time I reached Tyler, I was nearly running, just to get away from Tinker Bell. Deep breath. Be cool.

"Hey, Tyler." I yanked down the hem of my T-shirt and wrapped it around my index finger. For poise. "How's, uh . . . everything?"

"How's, uh . . . everything?" Did I really say that? And I want to win a Pulitzer. I can't believe I, Casey Smith, wordpainter, said that sentence.

But Tyler grinned. Grinned! "Casey . . . hi." He nodded at the baseball game. "You want in?"

In? My stomach sank as I realized what he meant. "No, no thanks. I couldn't. I can't. Not baseball. Definitely not baseball." I stammered.

This was not going well.

"You're kidding! Baseball *rules*! Here . . ." He took a few steps back and gently tossed the ball to me.

Panicked, I held out my arms as the ball sailed toward me. I cupped my hands. Closed my eyes. And—*thunk*. The ball landed in my hands.

A miracle.

"See?" Tyler flashed me an encouraging smile. "Anyone can play. It just takes practice."

My heart was pounding extra loud. Trying to ignore it, I plunged on. "Tyler, I need a favor. About your father? I need to interview someone from Riverhead. I'm writing a story for the school paper. And since your father works there . . . do you think he'd mind if I interviewed him?"

"Probably not. I'll ask him," he answered casually. He had no idea that this was going to make my story.

"Great. That's great." I hesitated. Should I mention that my class was visiting the mill tomorrow? Probably not. I was planning to keep a low profile during the tour. The anonymous student. "Can you talk to him soon? I'm on deadline."

"Sure," he said. "I'll ask him tonight."

Was he always this eager to help? Or was he doing me a special favor?

"You're up next, Tyler," called another boy. He came over and handed Tyler a batting helmet. "And keep your eye on the ball. Sam's losing control out there."

As Tyler headed over to the plate, the other guy turned to me. "Hey, Judy. How's it going?"

"It's *Casey*," I said through gritted teeth.

Now I recognized him. A tall, lean African American boy. Toothpaste-commercial smile. Warm brown eyes. Warm brown skin.

Gary Williams. We'd been in different classes in grade school, but we'd butted heads last year.

CASEY SMITH LOSES POETRY CONTEST—TO A BOY

I don't remember the details. Too painful. But the impression of Gary Williams—big ego, big mouth, big sneakers—still lingers.

"So . . . are you still writing poetry?"

Ouch. "Not much," I said, watching Tyler take

67

a swing. "I'm into journalism."

"Journalism?" Gary gazed over the field, adjusting his baseball cap. Sometimes he wears glasses—thin, round glasses that make him look smart. Overall, he would be cute. If he weren't so full of himself.

"Journalism," he repeated.

"You know—reporting the news? Newspapers?" I said encouragingly.

He rolled his eyes. "I *know* what it is, Judy. I'm just wondering where you're doing it."

"*Casey*. And it's for the school paper. *Real News*."

"I should try that. Not that I have time. There's baseball and basketball. And intramurals."

I looked him in the eye. He was fishing. I wasn't going to bite. At least, not the way he wanted. "Gary, did you make the football team this year?"

"No. But all my friends did," he said quickly. "And I'm going to sit with the team at the games. The coach wants me to study the defensive line."

"Gary," I said patiently. "Have you ever *played* for *any* team?" I already knew the answer, but it would be fun to see him squirm.

"No." He shrugged, then waved off my question. "No. But I've made it on to a few teams. Hey, I am the sports authority."

I shot a glance at my gym class. Tinker Bell was going to notice that I'd disappeared. I was about to turn back when it hit me.

The newspaper would need sports coverage. It wasn't my thing. I was willing to bet it wasn't Megan's thing. But sports was real news. Check any newspaper.

Gary was tied into sports at Trumbull. And if he'd beat me in a contest, the guy could write. *And*, as Megan had pointed out, we were desperate for staff.

"You know, Gary," I said, "maybe you should put together something for the school paper."

His eyes sparkled. "Definitely. Is this a tryout? Or am I in?"

I thought about Megan. It was only fair to give her some say about the staff. "Let's call it a tryout," I said. "Work up something about one of the teams, and get it to me by Thursday."

"Okay. A sportswriter!" He laughed. "This is great, Judy."

"*Casey*. And one more thing. The paper needs an editor. The staff gets to vote, but—"

"Oh, whoa!" He held up his hands. "Writing is one thing. But editor—I'm not sure I can take it on."

"Good thing," I said acidly. "Because it's going to be me. I'm the best person for the job." I was willing to give Megan some say about staff, but no way was I going to let her get Gary's vote. News is a cutthroat business.

"Of course." He nodded, his attention turning to a play on the field. "Who else could be editor of *Real News*?"

Did I mention that Gary is smart?

Reporter Sucked into Black Hole-in-the-Mall

AFTER SCHOOL I HEADED down to the dark gray cell for our staff meeting. A note was taped to the office door.

> *Dear Casey:*
>   *Do you mind if we meet at Hole-in-the-Mall? See you there at 3:15.*
> *Megan*

Did I mind? Of course I did!

Why meet in a burger place when we had an office? An office with computers that had been set up that very afternoon. I peered inside.

71

Light gleamed on one of the computer monitors. I was dying to try it out. I could almost hear it calling my name.

"Casey?"

No, that was Ringo, who was suddenly standing next to me.

"Hey, computers," he said. "Want to play Tetris?"

"It's not the computer club," I said. "They're here for the school paper."

Ringo squinted at Megan's note. "What's the Hole-in-the-Mall?" he asked.

"A burger place in the mall." I tore off the note and scrunched it up. "A hangout."

"Like a beach for people with no ocean."

"Sure. Take away the surfboards and sand. Add some booths, video games, and a soda counter, and you've got the picture," I said. Ringo's weird view was beginning to make sense. And that worried me.

"Way cool." Ringo hitched up the strap of his backpack, tucked his worn red spiral notebook under his arm and shrugged. "Let's go."

And that's how Ringo ended up at the *Real News* staff meeting. Not that I minded. In fact, I was getting used to having him around.

Hole-in-the-Mall was busy when we walked in. I scanned the cherry-red countertops and spotted Megan and Toni at a table in one corner.

Something about the Hole attracts kids. The noise, the name—I'm not sure. The entrance is a giant, ragged hole. And there's the usual flurry of high-school kids in checkered aprons, filling drinks and barking out orders over the booming music.

"Very un-mall," Ringo said, studying the memorabilia on the walls: A battered boogie board. A sombrero. A traffic sign that said NO OUTLET.

I pushed past two girls on Rollerblades to get to the table. I could barely see Megan over the big suggestion box. Had she lugged it all the way here?

Toni didn't glance up from contact sheets spread on her half of the table.

"Hey!" Megan said, smiling. "You made it."

"Why wouldn't I?" I snipped. Was Megan hoping I wouldn't make it?

Megan raised her eyebrows but didn't say anything.

I took a seat. "What are we doing here, anyway?"

Ringo pointed to me. "The universal question: What are we doing here? Who said that? Plato? Aristotle? Mr. Rogers?" Then he sat next to me.

I sighed. "Megan, Toni, meet Ringo. He's new in Abbington."

"Ringo?" Toni squinted at him. "You mean, like—"

"And you're here to work on the paper?" Megan couldn't contain her enthusiasm.

He shrugged. "I've done some origami. Does that qualify?"

"It's a *news*paper. For news. I told you that already," I said, trying to keep him on track.

"Got it. And I'm willing to work." He flipped open his notebook and started doodling again.

"Want to try an assignment?" Megan asked. She leaned over to peer in his notebook. "Maybe you've already written something that— Oh." Her voice dropped off when she saw that the page was filled with sketches—not words.

"Oh. Wow," Megan said, trying to cover her disappointment. "Those are . . . cute."

I shook my head in frustration. Let Megan run the meeting, and we'd be here when the mall closed. "Back to the beginning. Why aren't we in the office, Megan?"

"Toni has a baby-sitting job," Megan explained. "She's taking some kids to the movies—"

"In, like, ten minutes," Toni cut in.

"So I figured that the meeting would come to the staff," Megan finished.

"I am *not* the staff," Toni insisted. "You can use my photos. But no way am I working on a news-paper."

"Great." I frowned. "So we have two wanna-be editors."

"And one worker," Megan said, smiling at Ringo.

"A hungry worker." He stood up. "Anybody want anything?"

We shook our heads, and Ringo headed up to the counter to order some food. Real food. Why had I said no? It was against my code of ethics to interrupt a story meeting to scarf down a bucket of fries.

Maybe my code of ethics needed revising.

"I'm outta here, too." Toni stood up.

"But we haven't gone through the suggestions,"

Megan protested. "We haven't really done anything yet."

Toni just stacked the contact sheets and handed them to Megan. "Let me know if you need prints."

And she was gone.

"What a staff," I said, tickled at how Megan's meeting was falling apart. "Baby-sitting brats and space cadets ordering a bucket of burgers. Maybe you should talk to them about priorities."

Megan's blue eyes flashed with anger. "You know that saying? 'If you're not part of the solution, you're part of the problem?'" When I nodded, she added, "So what are you, Casey?"

That set me off balance. Megan had surprised me with a zinger. But I recovered fast.

"Right now I am a writer who's trying to get a newspaper going," I said quietly and, I hoped, with dignity. "Can we start?"

"Sure." Megan opened her backpack.

I peered inside. Talk about organized.

Her books were arranged neatly. Pens were clipped onto an inside pocket. Her pencils were sharpened and lined up in a clear plastic case.

No kidding.

Did she sort her paper clips by color? Did she carry around a mini-vac in case a pencil shaving broke loose and threatened the order of the Megan pack? I didn't get a chance to see before she took out a crisp sheet of paper and closed the bag.

"I had an idea that I worked on last night," she said. "A story explaining why we're bringing *Real News* back to life."

"I'll take that." I snatched the sheet from her and scanned a few paragraphs:

A VOICE THROUGH *REAL NEWS*

You're probably wondering, "Why do we need a newspaper?"

Because kids need a voice, that's why.

We receive information and orders from teachers and parents. Books and newspapers try to explain the world. Television and movies send us messages. Commercials explode with advice and persuasion. And the internet offers more than our brains could ever download!

But what about us? What about the way we feel? The thoughts we're thinking? The issues we're struggling with?

Kids need a voice . . .

That's why *REAL NEWS* is alive again.

Reading it, I got a funny feeling in my stomach.

The way Megan described all the information that pounds at us . . . the way she opened the door for kids to give feedback. It was *right*.

"There's something here," I finally muttered.

"Really?" Megan asked hopefully. She looked so pleased. Had perfect Megan been nervous about my reaction? "Do you think so?" Megan added.

I gritted my teeth. It was hard to say the words. But I had to. "You get the point across. And it's well written."

"Thanks, Casey." She smiled. Another sunny smile.

"We can talk about rewrites later," I said, sliding the sheet into my journal. "What about the rest of the paper?"

Megan shook the box excitedly. "It's almost full!"

"Wait—don't open it!" Ringo slid back into his seat, cradling a basket of fries. "I love presents. Whose birthday is it, anyway?"

"It's not a gift!" Megan smiled at him as if he were an adorable pet. Then she turned back to me. "Mr. Baxter told me about your idea to get suggestions from the kids in class. So I spoke to my English class, too."

"Oh, really?" I croaked. That made me nervous. What kind of spin had Megan put on her speech?

I crossed my fingers as she took off the lid and turned the box over.

Dozens of folded scraps of paper fell out onto the table.

"Whoa, it's like a piñata!" Ringo said, shoving another fry into his mouth.

I grabbed the closest piece of paper and read it.

WHAT ABOUT AN ADVICE COLUMN? THAT WAY, KIDS CAN GET ANSWERS TO THEIR PROBLEMS WITHOUT GETTING EMBARRASSED.

"An advice column?" I groaned.

"Advice is like the prizes that come out when a piñata breaks," Ringo said. "Advice showers down on you and you're sort of happy to pick it up. But when you look at it closely? Most of it is junk." Pulling a pen from the spiral of his notebook, he began doodling on a paper napkin.

I was too busy looking at the next suggestion to respond to Ringo. "Hey, here's one from someone who—"

I paused. It was intense. I read it aloud:

What about those kids who shoot other kids at school? Why do they do it? Are they full of anger? Or is something wrong with them? And could it happen to us? I think the whole thing is scary. Really scary.

The three of us were quiet for a minute.

Then another song began pounding out, breaking the moment. I put the paper in different spot on the table. The "good" suggestions pile.

"That's serious," Megan said.

"And a great idea," I added. "I guess I'm not the only one who realizes that world issues affect us. We need to do stories on violence and terrorism and—"

"Chemical warfare," Ringo added, and read:

Can someone really wipe out a whole city just by leaving an open jar of bacteria on a park bench?

Megan sighed. "I just . . . I just didn't think kids were interested in stuff like that."

"A lot of people underestimate kids, Megan," I said. I could afford to be generous. I was winning.

But as we read a few more, I began to lose my edge. A few of the suggestions curdled my stomach:

MY SUGGESTION

I would like to see a fashion section. Maybe something about what kids are wearing. Like when temporary tattoos were big? But not navel piercing. Because nobody's parents would let them.

Here's an idea.
How about a special spot for birthday wishes!?!

THINGS TO WRITE ABOUT

Things I would like to see in the school paper:

1. Poetry
2. Words from songs we like
3. A space for kids to complain about teachers who aren't fair and give out bad grades

I groaned. "We're definitely not wasting space on birthday greetings."

"I got a birthday card from my aunt Rita

once," Ringo put in. "With a parrot that sang 'Happy Birthday' when you opened it. It was the high point of my year."

Before I could say anything, I felt a change in the air—as if a new weather system had rolled into Hole-in-the-Mall. Turning around, I saw them.

A group of top jocks, breezing in the door.

As they headed toward a table in the middle of the Hole, I spotted Gary Williams at the group's epicenter.

My instinct was to ignore them. But I figured it was a good time to let Megan meet my new recruit.

"Gary!" I called out.

He sauntered over, with his hands in the pockets of his khakis. The expression on his face seemed to say, "Feel free to bow down and worship me."

Not me, bud. Though I couldn't say the same for Megan. Her eyes lit up when she spotted Gary.

"How's it going, Judy?" Gary asked casually.

"Casey," I muttered through gritted teeth.

He snapped his fingers. "Casey . . . right!"

"Gary, this is Megan," I said. "She's helping to get *Real News* started. Gary's working on a story, Megan. If it's decent, he'll be our sportswriter."

"That's fantastic!" Megan turned pink as she nodded at one of the guys Gary had come in with. "Isn't that Jason Milstein, from the eighth grade? Captain of the basketball team?" She was gushing, positively gushing.

Gary nodded and pulled a folded paper from his suede jacket. "I whipped this up on my laptop while the guys were in the locker room. A profile of Jason."

"Really? That's super!" Megan exclaimed, taking the paper like it was covered with gold.

"Yeah, well . . ." Gary adjusted his baseball hat over his baby dreads. "I work fast. And I'm tight with these guys. They'll give me the inside story on sports."

"Home run!" Megan crowed.

Gary laughed. A fake laugh. "Actually, in hoops, it's called a basket. He shoots, he scores!"

Megan covered her mouth. "Sorry." She giggled. But Gary looked at her as if what she'd said was, well, cute. *Somebody is going to have to explain guys to me one day. They can't be as stupid as they act, can they?*

Before Megan knelt down and kissed his Nikes, I jumped in. "Thanks, Gary. We'll get back to you . . . *after* we take a look at the story."

"Why wait? Have a seat, and we'll go over this right now." Megan smoothed out the pages of the story as Gary straddled a chair. She turned to me, adding, "And you went out and found us a sports-writer, Casey! Why didn't you say anything?"

What could I say? I'd figured that Gary's stories would be a draw for *Real News*. But how was I supposed to know that Megan would turn into pink mush just because a popular athlete was near?

Foul Odor Swallows
Three School Buses!

THE GOOD NEWS?

We made some serious decisions that afternoon. Megan, Gary and I agreed to edit each other for the first issue. Publishing without an editor is like flying a plane without a pilot. It's easy to crash and burn. Especially with Megan and me wrestling in the cockpit. Still, we mapped out a plan for the first issue of *Real News*:

PAGE 1: Pollution in the Sussex River—

Casey (YES!)

PAGE 2: Voice Through Real News—

Megan

Cafeteria Renovation—no takers yet

PAGE 3: Basketball Star Profile—Gary

First football game of season—Gary

PAGE 4: Editorials—Megan

Possible fluff piece on fashion, or

horoscope, or personal advice column???

The bad news?

"Page four is a joke," I told Megan.

"But we need to use some ideas from the suggestion box," she insisted.

Ringo and Gary had left a few minutes ago. I was stuck dealing with the Sugarplum Fairy. "And who's going to write these cotton-candy pieces?"

Pink stained Megan's cheeks as she smiled up at me. "I don't mind doing it."

I was ready to argue, but I bit my lip and shoved my journal into my backpack. The front page was mine. Did it matter if Megan printed hearts and flowers on page four?

Besides, I had work to do. If I didn't link Riverhead Paper to the dead fish studied by Project Green, I had no story at all.

"Remember, our deadline is Friday," Megan told me. "Your story stays on page one if you get the facts to back it up."

"No problem," I told her. Okay, it was a lie. A temporary lie, I hoped. My social-studies class goes to Riverhead tomorrow. And wasn't I just hours away from an inside interview?

When I got home, there was a message from the researcher for Project Green on our voice mail.

I listened to Dr. Dawn telling me to call her. I dialed the number right away, but got her machine.

"It's Casey Smith from *Real News*," I said into the phone. "I've got a tight deadline, Dr. Dawn. Please, call me as soon as you possibly can, okay? Thanks."

Gram was stacking salad greens on the counter as I hung up the phone. "Phone tag?"

I nodded. "How can they expect us to put out a paper if they don't even have phones in the office?" I waved a carrot for emphasis. "We should each have a cell phone."

"Definitely," Gram agreed. "And ask for chauffeured limos, while you're at it. Or helicopters."

I chomped on the carrot and swallowed. "Am I sounding like a spoiled brat?"

She smiled. "It's okay to dream. But sometimes the challenge of working around obstacles is half the fun."

I thought about that as I tramped into my

room and turned on my PC. There was an e-mail from Griffin that made me laugh.

To: Wordpainter
From: Thebeast
Re: total silence

Since you've been too busy to get back to me, I'll make it easy for you. Choose one of the following options.
STATEMENT: I have not responded to Griffin's messages because:
A. I spent the afternoon with the Kellehers and we got really close. A major bonding experience. In fact, I believe I am their missing triplet. Tomorrow the three of us will wear matching ribbons in our hair.
B. I'm swamped with work for the school newspaper.
C. Griffin who?

As I got on-line to update him, I realized how much had changed in less than a week. Just days ago I had traipsed down the halls of Trumbull thinking that my life was over. No Griffin. No newspaper. No fun.

And now my days were packed with people and stories and leads. I still missed Griffin. But something had changed.

To: Thebeast
From: Wordpainter
Re: Griffin Who?

Okay, Beast, back in your lair! The silence is broken. This hot tip just in—yes, I saw the K-twins today. No, we're not sharing temporary tattoos. But I admit, I was surprised when I saw them in action on the hockey field. Those two can hack around some hefty mud balls. . . .

I checked my backpack as our bus pulled into the lot at Riverhead Paper Wednesday morning. Pens. Tissue. Journal. I was ready to blow the lid off this mill. And not a moment too soon. Deadline was in two days. But we reporters work best under pressure.

Looking out the bus window, I saw the sprawling metal mill building. It gleamed in the sun—all glass and steel. It was bigger than it looked on the web site. Bigger. And a lot less friendly.

There was nothing much to see from the parking lot. Just the building and asphalt lot, which was surrounded by green grass and trees.

There was no sign of the waste pipes. In fact, you couldn't see the river at all, though I suspected it was on the other side of the tall evergreens that dotted one side of the parking lot. Behind the trees it looked like the land fell away into an embankment. But even that was hard to see.

All paths led into the glass entrance of the building. Intentional? You bet.

Hopping out of the bus, I found myself in front of an enormous flower bed. Someone had shaped the yellow mums into the letters "RP"—for River-head Paper.

Cute.

But not cute enough to cover up the horrible odor in the air. Something sour and nasty. Like sauerkraut.

"Casey?" It was Ringo. He shuffled over, his ever-present red notebook tucked under his arm.

I'd seen him wave from another bus back in the school lot just before we'd all left for the trip. I'd also noticed another familiar face on Ringo's bus—

Tyler McKenzie. So his class was assigned to the tour today, too. How lucky can one girl get?

Moving through the pack of kids, Ringo winced. "What's that smell?"

I sniffed to figure out what it was and started coughing instead. "It's *not* coming from those flowers."

Ringo covered his nose with the sleeve of his loose denim shirt. "I thought they made paper here. With sauerkraut on the side?"

"I bet it's coming from the river," I said.

"There's a river?" Ringo muttered in his sleeve.

"It's where the plant dumps chemicals." I took out my journal and started writing:

Wednesday, 10:21 A.M., Riverhead Paper

Creative landscaping. Probably designed to distract from the unsettling smell of chemicals pouring into the river.

Ringo turned toward the glass lobby doors. "Come on. I'm running for cover."

"I'll meet you in a minute," I said. Shoving my journal in my backpack, I stepped around the KEEP OFF THE GRASS sign and circled a tree. I wanted a firsthand look at the source of the sauerkraut smell.

"But Casey . . ." Ringo called.

"Casey Smith!" shouted another voice. I glanced back and saw Ms. Hernandez, my social-studies teacher. Her face was crumpled, annoyed. She thought I was trying to skip out on the tour. Ditch her class.

"Where are you going?" she added.

"I'll be right back!" I shouted, ducking behind a row of pine trees. I wasn't stopping now. Not when I was getting so close.

From there I had to hop a low hedge and circle a section of tall swamp grass.

Sort of a plant-life obstacle course.

I spotted the river ahead as someone else called, "Hey! Wait up!"

It was Tyler.

He tramped down the slope, catching up to me. "I'm supposed to bring you right back," he said.

A silly grin tugged at my lips. *Tyler* was coming after *me*. That had to mean something. I turned away to hide the goofy smile.

A barbed-wire fence blocked the way to the river, but I could see through to the water. Smelly water with brown sludge floating on top. I wished Toni was around to snap some photos.

I nodded at the mucky river. "It's disgusting."

"Yeah, this area is pretty bad," Tyler agreed. "But it starts to clear up a few yards away."

"You've been down here before?" I asked.

He nodded. "My father has to check the site. Sometimes, on weekends, I hang out with him."

"Did you ask him about the interview?" I asked.

"I did. He said okay. But he'd rather do it at home. If you could come over—"

"No problem," I said. "How's tonight?"

"Tonight is great." He glanced up the hill. "We'd better get back. Before they call out the Coast Guard."

Just then I noticed a small hill of ashen soil across the river.

"What's that? A moonscape?" I joked, pointing through the fence. It was a dry, bare mound of land. No grass. No trees. And the soil was glazed with a yellowish tint.

"Pretty weird, right?" Tyler nodded. "Actually, the guys that work here call it Bald Hill."

"You're kidding. Bald Hill?"

"There's something about the way the wind and water current carry the chemicals. It hits that hill, dead on. Nothing ever grows there."

"Now I know you're kidding!"

Tyler grinned at me as he trudged up the hill. "I've never seen anyone get so psyched about dirt."

"It's not just dirt," I explained, struggling to keep up with him. "It's proof that this plant is polluting the environment."

Tyler frowned. "Not really. I mean, it's just one hill. The rest of the area is in pretty good shape."

"And what about this awful smell?" I asked.

"It's worse than the dumpster behind the school cafeteria!"

"Casey!" Ms. Hernandez called as we climbed to the top of the embankment. "What were you thinking? I told the class to stick together."

"Sorry, Ms. Hernandez," I said. "But I needed a different perspective on the mill."

"Just stay with the group," she said, holding the lobby door as we walked in. I have a way of exasperating my teachers.

Tyler looked at me and smiled. "Don't worry," he said, "it smells a lot better inside."

My head was spinning as we joined the group. Tyler was being so . . . so *nice* to me. Not that it was a big deal. Okay, maybe it was a big deal.

And Tyler didn't seem worried about the chemicals here. The pollution thing didn't faze him. Maybe I was wrong about the mill. Maybe there really wasn't a story here.

"Hey, Tyler!" a guy with a buzz-cut motioned Tyler to join him as our group filed into a glass-walled corridor.

From here we overlooked the main room of the mill. The room was mondo huge, almost as long as a football field. In the center was a long trough of liquid. A mesh conveyor belt moved swiftly along the surface, carrying a mushy mix-ture of wood pulp and water.

Around the giant machine was a maze of platforms and stairways, all painted industrial gray. The same gray as our newsroom.

GRAY PAINT STRIKES AGAIN!
Uninspired Color Plagues Nation!

A tour guide joined us. I did a double take when she introduced herself as Ms. Dombrowski—the woman I'd talked to on the phone. She was youngish, with short brown hair and polished nails. She wore a tidy lavender suit and a teddy bear pin that Megan would envy.

I listened as Ms. Dombrowski explained the process: "The wood pulp is treated with chemicals to take out impurities and make the paper white."

I had learned this from my research. But seeing the machines in action gave me the total picture.

After the pulp was prepared, suction cups took the extra water out, and then the paper passed through cylinders to give it a smooth surface. From there the paper went through heated drying rolls. Whopping big ones. Think of a roll of paper towels that's bigger than a bus. Then the paper was cut into sheets or wound onto reels.

"Ms. Dombrowski?" I called out, pointing to a

series of pipes that fed into the trough. "Which chemicals are used in there? And what happens to the water when it's dumped back into the Sussex River?"

Her smooth smile never faltered. "Please save your questions for later. Now, if you'll all follow me. . . ."

Falling into step beside Ringo, I muttered, "I'm not going to let her give me the brush-off like that."

"No kidding. You don't even have any lint on you," Ringo said.

Ms. Dombrowski led our group to the next stop on the tour. We passed through a lounge area, with chairs, a copy machine and open doors that led to offices. Two people in coveralls stood next to the coffee machine. A guy wearing a shirt and tie was making copies at the Xerox machine right next to them.

Employees. A.k.a. inside sources.

The class moved on, but this was a chance I couldn't pass up. "Hi!" I said brightly. "My name is Casey Smith of *Real News*. How would you like to give me the inside story on paper?"

The workers looked at one another. Then one woman shrugged and said, "Sure. What do you want to know?"

I quickly flipped open my notebook and uncapped my pen. "What chemicals, exactly, are used to clean and bleach the paper?" I asked.

"Awesome. News in the making," I heard Ringo mumble. He picked up some scrap paper from the floor next to the copy machine and started doodling on it.

"Chemicals, huh?" the woman said. "Well, first off there's chlor—"

Someone touched my shoulder.

I turned around. "Um, hi, Ms. Dombrowski," I said.

"Didn't your teacher tell you to . . . stay . . . with . . . the . . . group?" Despite the smile plastered to her face, her words came out in angry bites.

"But—"

"The rest of the group is in the water-treatment facility," she interrupted. "Let's join them. Now."

I felt frustrated. I'd never get the information I needed through the standard tour. And that worker had been on the verge of giving me some answers!

But then Ms. Dombrowski's words sank in. "Water-treatment facility?" I echoed.

"We're getting warmer," Ringo said as we

reached the cavernous, gurgling room.

"Now, children," Ms. Dombrowski said, a note of condescension in her voice. What is it with grown-ups? Do we kids have "peanut-brain" tattooed on our foreheads?

"There is hazardous equipment in this area," she lectured, smoothing the lapels of her lavender jacket. "That's why I'm warning you again. Please, please—"

"Stay with the group," I finished for her.

Mill Grinds Healthy Trees into Smelly Sauerkraut!

OUR GROUP GATHERED at the base of two huge enclosed tanks that bubbled and hummed. Kids shuffled and joked about the rotten smell. This room was definitely the source of the sauerkraut. A man in orange coveralls paced on a platform next to the tanks as he addressed the class.

"This is the end of the production line," he explained. "The water-treatment tanks. In the other room you saw the bleachers, where the pulp is cleaned. And remember that big square container? That's the head box. There the pulp was mixed with water before entering the presses. These tanks are used to treat the excess water. We remove chemicals like bleach and dye before the water is returned to the environment."

Do you *really?* I thought. We would see about that.

"We've got technicians here seven days a week to make sure the water is clean when it's released into the Sussex River," he added.

My hand shot up. "Sir?"

He turned and smiled at me. "Yes?"

"Can you tell us what kind of bleaching agent Riverhead Paper uses?" I asked.

"We use chlorine," he announced. "The same chemical used to keep the water in swimming pools clean."

He made it sound harmless—even beneficial.

But I knew it wasn't that simple. "The chlorine isn't *totally* removed, is it?" I asked. "I mean, some toxic chemicals make it into the river, right?"

The technician shifted from one foot to the other. "Trace amounts of chemicals remain in the water. Trace amounts. But not enough to—"

"Kill the fish?" I interrupted him.

The technician frowned. Obviously annoyed.

Okay, maybe I shouldn't have interrupted him. But I was on a roll.

"And what about that hill across the river?" I continued. "The one where nothing can grow because of the chemicals carried over on the wind. I hear it's called *Bald Hill*."

There was a flurry of motion to my right. I turned and saw Tyler glaring at me. I'd deal with him later.

"And what about the river?" I pressed on. "Not that I have proof of pollution, but it's not looking too good. Actually, it isn't *smelling* too good, either."

A few kids snickered.

Again the technician looked annoyed as he turned back to me. He took a deep breath and lowered his voice. Was he trying to be patient? Or condescending? "All right. I'll be happy to answer your questions, Miss . . ."

"Casey Smith."

It was Tyler who supplied my name. His voice sounded tight . . . almost angry.

"Okay, Casey," the technician said. "Which question would you like me to answer first?"

I decided to catch him off guard and ask him a new question—*the* question. "Isn't it true this plant is dumping chemicals into the Sussex River?" I shot out.

But my attack didn't upset him. "As I said, trace amounts of chemicals make it into the water that's dumped out—the mill's emissions. But the government sets legal limits for the amount of chemicals we can release."

"And . . ." I probed. A journalist has to keep leaning on her source, hoping to find a crack. *The thin end of the wedge*, Gram likes to say. "Do you obey those limits?"

"Of course," he said. "It's the law."

"Do you have the emissions figures for Riverhead Paper?" I asked.

Ms. Dombrowski angled toward me. Ha! She didn't scare me.

"We test the treated water every three days to make sure it meets government standards," the technician said. "At that station, there."

He went over to an area with a sink and cabinets. "The chemical levels are monitored and recorded right here," he said, holding up a clipboard with papers.

Documents! My story needed some hard facts. And they were there on that clipboard. Squinting, I could see a graph with numbers and scribbles. But I couldn't make it out from here.

I cut through the group, heading through the narrow aisle between the two tanks. "Do you mind if I take a look?"

The technician held the clipboard out to me, but Ms. Dombrowski stepped in my way. "I'm sorry," she said. "But this is over the line."

Shrugging, the technician tossed the clipboard back onto the counter.

"Wait a minute!" I snapped at Mrs. Dombrowski. I wasn't going to let a cream puff in a purple suit stop my investigation. "What's the big deal about—"

"Official documents are confidential," Ms.

Dombrowski recited, as if quoting a manual. "This is a paper mill. A business."

"But I just wanted to see—"

"I'm sorry." Ms. Dombrowski stepped between the technician and me. There was nothing I could do.

Anger boiled through me—or was that the gurgling of the water-treatment tanks?

I stewed as she clapped her hands together. "Well, then. Looks like we're finished here. I'll be happy to answer any other questions when we get to the cafeteria. Thank you, Mr. Fielding."

The technician nodded as the class filed out of the room. Glancing back at the clipboard, I felt my story slipping through my fingers. I'd been so close. . . .

"Casey," Ms Dombrowski called from the door. "We're waiting."

I had to go. Crossing the narrow space between the tanks, I noticed a black security camera. It hung from the ceiling, and it was pointed right at me. I guess it was there to make sure no one was messing with the mix.

"Cheese!" I called, waving at the camera.

Then I followed the class to the cafeteria.

Tables were set with trays of donuts and cookies, and a screen had been set up for the film. Wednesday morning at the movies. Probably a dusty infomercial about the millions of ways people use paper.

As I reached for a donut, someone touched my arm.

It was Tyler. His brown eyes flashed with anger. "What was that all about?"

"I told you. I'm investigating a story." I was having enough trouble weaving a story together. The last thing I needed was Tyler turning against me.

"Investigating? Try *attacking*. You had your mind made up before that guy even had a chance to answer."

Okay, maybe I had come on strong with the technician. But Tyler was missing the big picture. If Riverhead was polluting the river, they were *wrong*. End of story.

"Look," I said. "It's for a story. If I don't get the facts, the piece is worthless."

"You didn't tell me you were out to trash Riverhead."

"That's not what I'm doing," I said hesitantly. I was on shaky ground. "I'm trying to get the facts. But if the facts prove that Riverhead is polluting the Sussex, I have to report it. It's what I do."

Tyler shook his head. "Sure. Well, good luck lining up an interview. There's no way you're getting near my father now." He turned and took off.

"Tyler, wait!" I ran to catch up to him.

Tyler stopped, but he didn't say anything. He just crossed his arms over his chest and stared at me.

I felt deflated. "Look," I said quietly. "Maybe I shouldn't have asked to interview your father. But I'm not trying to *trick* him—or anyone."

He shoved his hands into the pockets of his jeans. At least he hadn't walked away. I had one minute to make him understand.

"Okay, I pressed that technician," I admitted. "But there's a lot at stake here." Leaning closer, I added, "Like the Sussex River."

Tyler pointed toward the door. "Did you hear that technician? What part did *you* not understand? The water is cleaned before it goes back into the river. They check it every three days."

"There are still chemicals in it. Toxic stuff. But I don't have to tell you. You're the one who told *me* about Bald Hill!"

"I'm sorry I said that," he muttered.

"Why? Because it proves that something is wrong here?" This was a side of Tyler I didn't like. An ostrich with its head in the sand. "This mill is polluting. And the people who work here know it. They even make jokes about it!"

He shook his head. "They follow the legal limits."

"How do you know that?" I pressed.

Tyler paused. "Okay. So what if you're right and the mill is polluting the river? What do you want them to do? Stop making paper?"

"No, no, no." I waved my hand. "There are ways of making paper that don't pollute as much." I'd read all about this on the internet. "Some mills have installed computerized controls now. And they use recycled material. Or a chlorine-free bleaching agent."

"And all those things cost more, right?"

I shrugged. "Sometimes."

"Okay. What if all paper mills do what you're saying, and the price of paper doubles. And it costs twice as much to print the school newspaper. *Your* paper."

I shook my head. "It doesn't have to—"

"Changes cost money," he snapped. "So what would you do then? Print the school paper on a banana peel?"

My face felt hot. I was probably red from my nose to my perfect pink ears. How could Tyler be so stubborn—so stupid about this?

"There's no middle ground here," I told him. If they're polluting, it's wrong. End of story."

This time when he turned and walked away, I let him go. He was wrong. So wrong! And I was more determined than ever to prove it.

Camera-Shy Reporter Meets Jaws of Death

I SNAGGED RINGO as he picked up a donut. "Empty calories," he said. "Is that because there's a hole in the middle?"

"You'd better take it to go," I said, handing him a napkin. "We're skipping the film."

"We're going somewhere?" Ringo asked. He tucked two donuts into a napkin and balanced them on his notebook. They started to slide away. I grabbed them.

"We'll talk as we go." I shoved the wrapped donuts into my backpack and scanned the room for Ms. Dombrowski. She sat at the other end of the cafeteria, schmoozing with the teachers.

Time to make our move.

As Ringo and I made our way down a corridor,

I tried to explain things. "You saw the way Ms. Dombrowski cut that interview short," I told him. "That employee was talking and—*WHAM!*—it was over."

"Yeah. She's not very social," he said.

A woman in coveralls passed us. I held my breath, waiting for her to stop us, but she just moved on.

"And now Tyler won't let me talk to his father," I told Ringo when she was out of earshot. My thoughts were scattered, but Ringo seemed to be following along. "And I was so close to that emissions chart, I could taste it."

"Now *that's* empty calories," Ringo said.

"And it really bothers me that Tyler doesn't get this whole thing," I went on. "Like I'm being unreasonable. Me—unreasonable!"

"As if," Ringo said.

"I've got to prove him wrong," I said.

"Definitely," he agreed. "So where are we going?"

"Back to the water-treatment room. To check those emissions levels."

Ringo paused mid-step. "You lost me. What do you think you'll find?"

I frowned. "Okay, maybe there's nothing there. On the other hand, maybe those charts will lead to something. Are you coming?" I asked, pointing down the corridor.

Ringo shrugged. "Sure. I hear the film they're showing is a dog."

We made it to the water-treatment room without attracting any attention. I peeked through the doorway and whispered, "We're in luck." The place was deserted. "Everyone must be on break."

Opening the door, I hung back to check out the ceiling. There was just the one security camera I'd noticed before. "Okay," I said, "if we want to stay off camera, we have to avoid that narrow aisle between the tanks."

I stepped into the sour-smelling room, motioning for Ringo to follow.

Now that we were alone, the sounds of our footsteps echoed off the concrete floor, giving a hollow, damp sound. The machinery twisted and gleamed—a metal monster.

The treatment tanks hummed, reminding me of what was inside. Toxic chemicals.

Definitely eerie.

"Don't get too close to those things," I warned Ringo.

"Don't worry." He edged toward one wall, hugging his notebook. "I keep expecting some monster to rise out of there. The creature from the pulp pits."

Straight ahead were the two tanks, separated by the narrow aisle. The testing station was on the far end of that aisle—along with the report I needed.

And the entrance to that aisle was guarded by that darned security camera.

"How are we going to get those charts without stepping into camera range?" I said, thinking aloud.

"Cut over that way?" Ringo suggested, pointing to the right.

There was a wide, shallow pool with a narrow walkway that ran around it.

We headed over and paused. Metal tubing looped over the side of the tank. There were wires. Meters. Valves. A lot of things to trip over.

Next to the walkway was a red DANGER sign.

"Okay," Ringo admitted. "Bad idea."

I looked to the opposite end of the room. There were no windows. And no place to squeeze between the tank and the far wall.

We were stuck. And the reports I needed were just a few yards away.

So close. So far.

An EXIT sign glowed eerily in the shadows. *Two* EXIT signs. One on our side of the tanks. The other near the testing station. Hmm.

Could I duck outside, then cut back in through the EXIT door by the testing station?

"That's a possibility," I murmured. Staying

out of camera range, I went over to the EXIT door near me.

I jumped up to look out the high glass window and saw a flash of green grass.

"Yes!" I jumped up again. Outside, the green lawn stretched along the side of the building toward the other EXIT door. "Yes!"

"Go, Casey!" Ringo said, springing up beside me. "Isn't it great that you can do aerobics anytime, anywhere?"

"I don't exercise." I frowned. "But I found a way around that camera. I can cut out this door, run along the outside of the building and pop in that door," I said, pointing to the EXIT SIGN beside the testing station.

"Cool." Ringo grinned. "But that door might be alarmed. Or what if it's locked from the outside?"

"Good point." I touched the smooth metal bar on the door. "But usually there's a sign to warn people. We'll just have to chance it."

I turned to Ringo. "You stay here. The door might lock behind me."

Ringo looked around nervously. "Okay, Casey. Just make it quick."

I felt charged up. This was the way I wanted to investigate a story. Danger. Peril. Adventure. But Ringo didn't look nearly as enthusiastic.

"Nervous?" I asked.

"Definitely."

"Well, here goes." Hitching up my backpack, I pushed on the bar.

No alarm sounded.

Relieved, I pushed open the door and stepped out. "This is going to be easy. Just stay there and be the lookout."

"The lookout." Ringo nodded, holding the door ajar with his foot.

"Right." The grass felt wet under my hightop sneakers as I backed away.

Then his face went pale. "Look out!"

"What?"

A low growl tore through the air as I swung around. A blur of teeth and fur and menacing eyes was coming right at me.

Studies Prove Donuts Solve Most Problems

"WHOA!" I froze in place.

The dog pounded to a halt at my feet and growled.

It was a German shepherd. All teeth and gums—

Ready to tear into a juicy ankle. My ankle!

Don't move. Don't panic, I told myself. I knew dogs could smell it when people were afraid. Well, right now this beast was getting a noseful. Then again, was it able smell anything besides the stench from the river?

"Hey, bud," Ringo spoke to the dog from the doorway. "Did we scare you? I know you scared us."

Snarling, the dog stood its ground.

"In my backpack," I muttered, too afraid to

113

move. "The donuts."

"I sort of lost my appetite."

"For the dog!"

"Oh." Ringo's gray eyes never shifted away from the dog as he put down his notebook and slowly unzipped the pack on my back. I held my breath as he handed me the wrapped donuts. The dog's growls went up a notch.

"Hey, boy, are you hungry?" I asked the dog.

It barked.

Was that good? I wasn't sure. Moving slowly, I placed a donut on the ground. "Help yourself."

The dog barked again.

Its beady eyes glared, checking us out. Then it leaned down, sniffed the donut and gulped it up.

"Pretty good, huh?" Ringo cajoled the dog. "I bet you're sick of kibble and bones. Right, bud?"

The dog licked its teeth and barked. A friendly bark. Ringo put out his hand and let the dog sniff it. The dog licked Ringo's palm and wagged its tail.

I handed Ringo the other donut. "You keep the canine happy. I've got to check those charts."

Ringo sat cross-legged against the open EXIT door. The pooch was nosing around him, trying to find the second donut that Ringo was hiding behind his back. It completely ignored me as I moved away.

It was a short trip around the side of the building. I scurried through the grass to the other door—which wasn't locked.

My luck was holding.

I pushed through the door and popped back into the testing room and went over to the station.

"How's it going?" I called to Ringo.

He slouched in the open doorway, the dog resting by his side. "Okay. I just wish we had more food."

The clipboard still sat on the counter. My fingers closed around the smooth edge. At last—all secrets would be revealed.

I lifted it up. I read it. But the chart was a riddle—all symbols and numbers.

I didn't recognize the symbols for most of the chemicals listed. But I was pretty sure "Cl" was chlorine. I started copying the data into my notebook, figuring I could check it later against the information I had at home. I was about to flip to the page below, when something caught my eye.

"The date," I murmured.

"What?" Ringo called from the doorway.

"This reading was taken over three months ago!"

"Um, Casey?"

I was too busy flipping through the sheets to

pay attention to him. "Look at these! They're *all* older than three months," I said. "What about all the readings that should have been taken between then and now? Why aren't they here?"

"Casey," Ringo said again. "Someone's coming!"

That got my attention.

Grabbing the clipboard, I bolted toward the EXIT near the testing station. "Outside!" I called to Ringo. "And take Lassie with you!"

Plunging through the door, I darted across the grass. Ringo and the dog met me just outside the other EXIT door.

"Don't panic," I said. "Just stay low and keep quiet. When they don't see us, they'll go away."

"Maybe," Ringo said. "But if it's the technicians, back to work, we'll be stuck out here for hours."

He was right. "Give me a boost and I'll take a look."

Ringo squatted down so that I could step on his bent knee. Pressing against the door, I peered through the high window.

There was a flash of lavender—

Ms. Dombrowski's lavender suit.

"Down! Down! Down!" I whispered.

"What is it?"

"Ms. Dombrowski."

Ringo slumped against the wall and sighed. "And we know who she's looking for."

I held my breath. Her heels clicked on the cement floor.

Ringo hunkered down beside me.

Had she seen me peeking in?

Please, go away, I pleaded silently.

The footsteps paused.

I panicked.

Then she moved off. The footsteps faded.

Ringo hoisted me up again. "She's still inside—across the room," I said, dropping to the ground. "While we're waiting, I'll get to work."

"Here?" Ringo asked, ruffling the dog's fur.

"I can't take these charts with me. But I want to copy some info—just in case." I took out my notebook.

Ringo gasped. "Notebook!"

"Yes. And pen," I said, holding up a felt tip pen.

"No! *My* notebook. I left it inside."

I winced. "Well, she didn't seem to notice it. Maybe we'll get lucky."

Huddled against the building, I jotted down the chemical levels into my notebook. Beneath the figures, I wrote a question:

???Where are the emissions reports from the last 3 months???

"That's it for now." I closed my notebook, then

stood up. This time I jumped up to peer in the window.

"She's gone."

Ringo sighed. "Good. Let's get out of here."

"Just give me a minute," I said, running off to the other EXIT door. I popped inside, returned the clipboard to the testing station and sprinted back to Ringo and the dog.

Ringo kneeled. The dog nuzzled his denim shirt.

"Yeah, me too," he told the dog. "Thanks for everything, bud."

We opened the EXIT door—no one in sight.

The dog barked good-bye as we eased inside, closing the door behind us.

"Okay." I took an excited breath. We had gotten some information. Maybe even a clue. And no one would ever know. "Let's get back to the cafeteria."

Ringo checked the floor, scurrying around the doorway. "Hey . . . my notebook." He frowned. "It's gone."

"Is this what you're looking for?"

My heart jumped at the strange voice.

A lavender suit stepped out from behind a tank. Ms. Dombrowski! Ringo's red notebook was in her hand.

Busted.

Dreaded Spots
Plague Newsroom

As THE BUS rolled back to school, I jotted a few things down in my journal.

BREAKING THE RULES ON THE MILL TOUR—

Advantages:

1. I copied info from emissions reports.

Consequences:

1. Our teachers are ticked off.

2. Ms. Dombrowski is threatening to cancel future tours. (I don't believe her.)

3. I had to leave Riverhead Paper without finding out <u>why</u> there were no emissions reports for the last three months.

4. Ringo is worried that Bud-the-dog might be punished for fraternizing with the enemy.

Overall, the situation wasn't that bad.

But I did feel sorry for the dog.

And I wondered about those missing reports all through my afternoon classes.

What did it mean? Did someone hide the reports because the emissions levels were too high? Did the technicians stop testing the water over the past few months? Or did someone just make a mistake and stick the recent reports in the wrong place?

Those missing charts were still on my mind when I showed up for our staff meeting after the final bell.

I walked into the newspaper office and blinked.

"Why am I seeing spots?" I asked.

Polka dots.

They covered the shiny top of a big round table. They bounced on the seats of the stools around it. Stools that really stood out, from their speckled vinyl to their lime-green legs.

"Do you like it?" Megan ran a hand over the table-top, beaming. "I found it in my grandmother's attic.

Gary and Jason helped me move it here last night."

"Isn't it great?" Gary piped up from behind a computer screen.

"It's . . . *bright*," I said, still a little dotty.

"I knew we needed a work table," Megan went on. "And Grandma didn't want it anymore. So . . . here it is!"

"Here it is," I repeated, dropping my journal onto a desk.

"Do you like it?" Megan asked. "The truth."

"The truth—it's hideous," I admitted. "But we do need a table. And it'll be okay with a can of paint."

"Paint over the spots?" Megan's brows lifted. "But that's the best part."

"Hey!" Ringo skidded in the door with a huge grin. "Dalmatian Station! I love it."

"Yeah." Gary's fingers tapped at the keyboard. "Megan's really pulling this thing together."

Ringo patted the tabletop. It wobbled. "I love old things," he said. He patted down his jeans, then took a folded wad of paper out of the pocket of his denim shirt. Tucking it under one rickety leg, he smiled. "There. Nice and steady."

"Okay," I went on, trying to ignore the speckled furniture. "On to editorial." I handed Megan her article on the rebirth of *Real News* and collapsed in a chair to stew. The newspaper was slipping through my fingers . . . right into Megan's meticulous hands.

Everyone loved her sense of fun. They loved her spotted table. They were on her side. It was time to remind everyone that I was their best choice for editor.

"You know, guys," I said, "maybe we should move up the election. If we're going to put a masthead in our first issue—you know, the list that tells everyone who does what on the paper—we need to vote now."

"Oh, we're not going to vote until next week," Megan said casually. "There's too much going on now. We can live without a masthead."

"Wait a second." I turned to her. "When did we decide that?"

"I don't know . . . sometime yesterday?" She gave me a thoughtful look. "Or at lunch today?"

And where had I been?

Researching my story at the library. On the phone. At the mill.

"Somewhere between choosing typeface and sketching a layout," Gary added. "Although we've been having serious trouble with Disktop." This was the desktop publishing software the school had given us for layout. "I've never used it before."

"I'll take a look," Ringo said. "I used to work on Disktop at my mom's office."

As he sat down beside Gary and clicked into

the program, I felt very alone. Things had been going on in this office. Choices had been made.

All without me.

I'd been so busy working on my story, I'd missed the chance to lay the paper's foundation. That bothered me. I knew that the choices had to be made to print the paper in time. But that didn't make me feel any better.

Megan came over and stood in front of my desk. "Casey. Got a minute?"

Cautiously I glanced up at her. Did she sense my feelings? Was she going to try to soothe my wounds?

There's nothing I hate more than pity.

"I'd like to run this beside Toni's collage. Maybe call it 'Portrait of the Artist.'" She handed me a piece of paper.

Who is the person behind the camera? Meet Toni Velez, our staff photographer. In a recent interview, *Real News* staffer Megan O'Connor found out what makes Toni tick:

M: Where did you live before you came to Abbington?

T: Well, my dad is in the military. We've always moved around a lot. You name the place, I've

123

probably lived there. Plus, all my relatives live far away. They're in Mexico.

M: Do you visit them often?

T: Not really. At first I wrote a lot of letters. Then I started taking pictures so I could have a way of staying in touch with them.

M: Isn't it hard, changing schools and friends so often?

T: You get used to it. Anyway, my dad decided to retire from active service so we could settle down. Now he teaches at Phillips Military Academy. So I'm stuck here.

M: Don't you like Abbington?

T: It's okay. But I'm ready to move on. I'm used to taking pictures of pyramids and glaciers and castles. Compare that to Trumbull. I'm supposed to line up kids on the debating team and take their picture? And everyone has attitude. It's hard to get excited about a shot like that.

I thought of Toni, girl of a thousand rings, wild hair, wilder tongue. Something in her profile hit me.

The way she felt stuck here in Abbington . . .

I understood that. The feeling that this school—this town—this state!—wasn't big enough for me. That I was stuck here. At least until I worked my way out. Funny how you always think you're the only one who feels different, out of step, on the outside looking in. I wonder. Is it possible that *everyone* feels this way sometimes?

Did I have more in common with Toni than I'd thought? After all, we both had boom-chicka-boom. Food for later thought.

I finished the interview and handed it to Megan.

"This works," I told her. "It will give the whole collage a theme. It pulls the photos together."

"Do you think so?" Megan's eyes lit up.

Just then Mr. Baxter bustled in, saving me from being prodded for more praise. He was lugging his briefcase and jacket. "This will be a seven-minute meeting," he said, checking his watch. "My daughter has a soccer game, and I'm already late."

"But Toni isn't here yet," Megan pointed out.

"Because she keeps insisting that she's not on the staff," I told Megan. "Just give up already."

"She'll be here," Megan said firmly.

"You can bring her up to speed when she shows up." As Mr. Baxter straddled a chair, he turned and pointed at me. "Casey Smith. I was just talking to Ms. Hernandez about you."

Uh-oh. Trouble. "She's mad," I said. "Right?"

"She's concerned," Mr. Baxter answered. "And I don't blame her. Do you know what happens to students who wander off during field trips?"

I could only guess. "Detention? Suspension? Life in prison?"

He cracked a smile. "They are usually banned from other field trips. That would cramp your style, wouldn't it?"

"Mr. Baxter, you don't know the whole deal. I was researching a major story. A pollution scandal involving Riverhead Paper."

"Really?" Mr. Baxter seemed impressed.

"Wait a minute," Megan said. "Casey's story is still a little . . . light on facts."

"Not anymore," I insisted. "Mr. Baxter, have you seen that place? The river is a mess. The whole area stinks."

Mr. Baxter nodded. "I'll look forward to reading about it. Just make sure you have the facts to back it up. Otherwise, we'll have to go with a backup story," he said.

"No, no!" I insisted. "My story will be ready."

Megan glanced at me uneasily. "Casey, I'd like you to think about what happened today. You broke rules. You took risks. You dragged poor Ringo into it."

"'Poor Ringo' had the time of his life," I said. "Anyway, he's a free agent." What was Megan's problem? Was she auditioning for the role of schoolmarm in the next play?

"Hello?" Ringo called from the PC, where he was still trying to unscramble Disktop. "Don't talk about me like I'm not here. The truth is, I sort of liked the adventure. And I definitely liked the dog."

"The point is," Megan said, "Casey's behavior reflects on all of us. And it reflects on the paper." Her blue eyes squinted at me. "We can't put ourselves in dangerous situations."

"Oh, right," I said. "And I'm never going to cross the street. Or use a knife. I promise I'll never bite into a hot pizza without blowing on it first."

I should have remembered Megan had no sense of humor. She didn't laugh. No one laughed. All eyes were on Megan, who was sucking the energy from the room. The intense expression on her face said that she was serious.

Dead serious.

Beanies and Weenies Make Front Page!

SHEESH. All I did was sneak around a paper mill. Was that a felony?

"Some news stories don't fall into your lap, Megan," I said. "You have to chase them. You jump off a cliff and grab them on the way down."

"Let's hope that won't be necessary," Mr. Baxter cut in. "Can we move on?"

"But Mr. Baxter," Megan protested. "Casey has to realize—"

"Journalists approach things differently," Mr. Baxter said, glancing at his watch.

Score one for me, I thought.

"And I have to go," Mr. Baxter went on. "What's your plan for the layout?"

Mr. Baxter's cut-to-the-chase tone defused the tension. For now.

Her lips puckered in annoyance, Megan handed over sample layouts, a fat stack of stories and a list of stories we wanted to run.

Leaning over Mr. Baxter's shoulder, I eyed the list:

```
PAGE 1:
LEAD: Mill Polluting Our River
(Casey)
   OR Cafeteria Face-lift (???)


PAGE 2: A Voice Through Real News
(Megan)
   Alfred Trumbull: Who Was He?
Who Cares? (Casey)


PAGE 3: Final Innings for Trumbull
Baseball (Gary)
   Jason Milstein: A Force on the
Court (Gary)
   Surviving Intramurals—and Liking
It! (Gary)


   PAGE 4: Just Do It: School
Activities (Megan)
   Fashion Fads (???)
   Milstein (cont'd)
```

PAGE 5: Beauty Pageants: Pretty?
Says Who? (Casey)
    Should Smoking Be Allowed at
School? (Megan)
    Teacher of the Week??? (???)
    Cyber Space (????)

    PAGE 6: JAM Advice Column
(Megan)
    Collage of Student Styles (Toni)
    Photographer Profile (Megan)

I was very pleased that two of the stories I'd done over the summer had made it in. Even better, the paper had gone from four pages to six. Already, we'd grown.

Then there was the layout, which showed how pages two and three, which face each other, would look. Of course, the words on the page didn't make sense. The sample was just to give an idea of how the paper might look.

The type was bold but not too flashy. The layout looked neat and eye-catching. But it still bothered me that so many decisions had been made without me.

"I like this," Mr. Baxter told Megan. "You've set up a solid framework."

Watching him stuff the papers into his brief-case, I felt a twinge of annoyance. Because he was right.

"I'll give you my feedback in the morning," Mr. Baxter said. "But you need to keep going. Input and edit and proofread your stories. We're up against a killer deadline."

"Deadline." Ringo was thoughtful. "So you're dead if you don't make it over the line in time, right?"

I rubbed my temples. Ringo was looping again.

Toni came in with copies of photos just as Mr. Baxter was leaving. "I can't stay," she said. "The copy machine jammed. And Ms. Kiegel is a royal pain."

Mr. Baxter slid the copies into his bag and told Toni, "Next time, tell her you're with me."

"I did!" Toni insisted. "Anyway, those copies will give you an idea of the photos we want to publish."

"We'll talk in the a.m.!" Mr. Baxter called, sweeping out the door.

That left Megan and Toni and Ringo and Gary and me. We all started talking at once. Then I held up a hand and let out a whistle.

"Okay, guys, let's keep moving," I said.

"I gotta go," Toni said.

"Can't you stay?" Megan asked. "We could use some help on the computer. And you're good at that stuff."

Toni rolled her eyes.

I couldn't figure this girl out. Did she just want to be coaxed? Or did she have an overdose of attitude? Forget about our being similar. She was nothing like me. Well—except maybe for the attitude part.

"The point is, are you on the staff or not?" I pressed. When Toni glared at me, I added, "Because we need your help. *If* you have the time."

Letting out a sigh, Toni slid her bag onto the floor and sat down beside Ringo.

Score another one for me, I thought. "What else do we need to assign?" I asked Megan.

She ran a finger over her list. "There's the piece about the cafeteria. And these special features. 'Teacher of the Week.' 'Fashion Fads. . . .'"

I groaned. "I guess we have to put some fluff in."

"Sure we do," Ringo pointed out. "*Real News* should be like a salad bar. There's something for everyone."

"Whatever," I muttered. "Just count me out for the moment. I need to get more info about Riverhead Paper."

Like what had happened to those three months' worth of charts. Who had removed them? And why?

I came back to earth and realized the other kids were talking about something else now.

"The cafeteria renovation was a big deal for Trumbull," Gary said. "Everyone says it was a slop pit. I say we go with it for the front page. No matter what."

"Come on, Gary. The cafeteria? That's not news," I scoffed.

"It's not a major scandal," Megan admitted. "But it *is* news, and if your Riverhead story doesn't work, we'll need it. I'll work up a draft."

I couldn't believe she could mention major pollution in the same breath with new linoleum. On the other hand, if my story got axed, "Adventures in Beanies and Weenies!" was going to be the front-page story. And the front-page story, whatever it was, was going to have my name on it.

"Okay," I said. "I'll write the cafeteria story."

I wrote a few sentences about the new look of the cafeteria, then ran out of steam. This story would need research, too. Boring research. Chats with cafeteria staff and painters who'd slapped yet another coat of institutional beige on the walls.

I decided to knock off my science homework first. Opening my textbook, I started reading about volcanoes.

Ringo and Toni left. Megan said good-bye, too. There really wasn't anything to do until we heard back from Mr. Baxter. Only Gary stayed, his eyes glued to a tiny TV he'd brought in. My mind drifted from my homework to my story. My *real* story.

Seeing the mill had given me some visuals. I knew the smell of the place and the description of Bald Hill would connect with readers. But how could I prove that Riverhead Paper was polluting the river?

Flipping through my textbook, I saw a picture of a volcanic explosion. I flipped to a photo of a crew on a boat testing ocean water for volcanic matter.

Testing the water. Testing the water! That was it!

I shoved my books into my backpack. I could get the litmus paper from our science lab. One dip in the water would tell me if the acidity of the water was too high. "I'll test the water myself!"

"The pool is closed, Casey," Gary said absently. The roar of fans blasted out of the TV. "Swim team practices in the morning."

"I'm talking about the Sussex River," I told him. "Somehow I've got to get near those pipes. . . ."

I pictured Riverhead Paper in my mind. There was that embankment . . . and the area around the river was fenced off. A barbed-wire fence. No, I would have to cross over from the far bank. . . .

"I need a boat," I said.

"Boat?" Gary pulled his gaze away from the TV. "You name it, my family's got it. You should check out our speedboat. Fifty miles an hour on the lake. Plus, we've got canoes, kayaks, sailboats—"

"Do you know how to drive them?" I interrupted.

"Sure. I'm not supposed to mess with the engines. But the kayaks and sailboats are fair game. Do you sail?"

"No," I said. "But I need a boat."

And apparently he had plenty to spare.

"What for?" he asked.

"I'll tell you on the way." Slinging my backpack over my shoulder, I stood up. "Let's go, Gilligan."

Canoe Sucked into Whirlpool of Waste!

"WATCH YOUR POSTURE, CASEY," Gary told me. "You can't get a full paddle stroke if you're all stooped over like that."

"I'm not stooping," I yelled. My knuckles were white from clenching the paddle. "I'm holding on for my life!"

We had just launched his family's shiny aluminum canoe into the Sussex, upriver of Riverhead Paper. I sat in the front of the canoe, while Gary manned the back.

I figured we had about an hour and a half before the sun set. More than enough time to get close to the pipes and dip the litmus paper into the river. No problem.

Except I had never noticed how dark and gurgling and *fast* this river was. And the yellow life vest I wore was little comfort. In fact, it was annoying. Why didn't they design these things for girls?

"Gary?" I clutched my paddle with one hand, the edge of the canoe with the other. "How deep do you think the water is?"

"Not more than ten or twelve feet," Gary said, as if that was nothing at all. "Actually, it's not the depth that's a challenge. It's the current. It can really pull you along."

"Maybe we should go back," I said.

"Come on! This is nothing compared to the rapids out west," Gary said, dipping his paddle. "The whitewater really churns."

I thought of the muck around the shoreline at the mill. What if the current pulled us into the toxic waste? Yuck. My stomach did a complete flip.

"The water's not the only thing churning," I mumbled.

I looked longingly back at the shore. Gary's older brother waved from the blue station wagon he had used to drive us and the canoe to the river. I didn't dare let go of anything to wave back.

"You need to hold the paddle with *both* hands, Casey," Gary said. "One hand holds the top. Use the other to grip the shaft near the blade."

"This isn't a sport. It's a death wish!" I snapped.

"*You're* the one who wanted to test the water," Gary reminded me.

He was right. And I still wanted to do it. But I had pictured us gliding across the river. Not shooting the rapids like a pinball.

At least Gary knew what he was doing.

Somehow we made it across the river. The next thing I knew, our canoe was approaching the three round pipes.

The mill loomed over us at the top of the hill. The water here was mucky and smelly. It didn't look to me like anything was being "cleaned" or "treated."

"Is this close enough?" Gary asked.

"Yes," I said, "but is there any way to steady the canoe while I lean over the side?"

He looked around, then pointed into the shadowed bushes. "See that dock?" A short wooden pier jutted out into the water. A sign warned: NO TRESPASSING! PROPERTY OF RIVERHEAD PAPER. "We can use that."

With smooth strokes Gary paddled toward the dock. "You know," he said, "when you told me about this assignment, you didn't mention the smell."

"I must have forgotten," I lied, reaching under

the life vest to the pocket of my jacket. I yanked on a plastic glove and took out a litmus strip. I'd had no problem getting the testing stuff from the science lab. My teacher, Ms. Strader, had even been interested in my story. Of course, I'd had to listen to her explanation:

"Litmus paper reacts to acid by turning colors. In this case, blue," she'd said, handing me the strip and the color key. "The shade of that color indicates the level of acid in the water." All I needed to do was dip and compare the strip to the spectrum on the key, which showed eight different shades of blue. She had pointed to the darkest shades, adding, "Anything in this range is toxic."

But I knew "toxic" wasn't enough.

Back to my research. Using the computer in the newsroom, I clicked on the Project Green web site. There was a list of different chemicals—types of industrial waste. Also listed were the legal limits of those chemicals.

Checking those limits against the percentages of acid marked on the color key, I found the answer. The three darkest bars of color indicated percentages that were above legal limits.

Bottom line, if the litmus strip turned dark blue, I had a story. A blow-your-socks-off story.

If only Gary could steady this darned canoe . . .

"Would you dock the boat, already?" I snapped, gripping the litmus paper. No way was I leaning over the side while this boat kept wobbling in the water.

"Easy, skipper," he said. "The current's stronger than I thought over here."

The canoe lurched as he reached toward the dock. At last he grabbed a post.

"Steady as she goes," he said smugly.

Don't you hate it when boys refer to things as "she"? I bristled. But there was no time to argue. Time for the big test.

Using my gloved hand, I dipped the strip into the water. I swished it around three times. Then once more for good luck. At last, I lifted the strip . . .

And saw a flash of blue.

Deep, dark blue. Similar to the darkest band of blue on the key.

Yes! I wanted to jump up and cheer.

This was the proof I needed. Riverhead was dumping illegal levels of poison into this river.

Suddenly I heard barking.

Loud, angry barking. And it was getting closer every second.

I gasped when I caught sight of two German shepherds loping toward us down the steep slope. They strained against their leashes, which were held by two guards in brown uniforms.

"Guards!" Gary cried.

"We've got to get out of here," I said, shoving the color key into my jacket pocket. I went to pull the glove off, and the litmus strip slipped out of my hand.

"Whoa!"

As I reached for it, the strip fell against the rim of the boat . . . then over the side . . .

Back into the water.

"No!" I yelped. "My proof! I need it!" I lunged over the side and the boat tipped. My fingers reached out over the mucky water as the blue strip of paper was swept away.

"Casey!" Gary was paddling like crazy. "Stop it! You're going to dump us both in the water."

"But I dropped the—"

"Shut up and paddle!" Gary yelled.

I stuck my paddle into the water, but it didn't seem to help.

"What are you doing!" Gary growled. "You're steering us back to the dock!"

Just then the front of the canoe banged against the end of the dock. Hard.

"Whoa!" I gulped as the canoe tipped.

I grabbed onto the dock to steady it . . .

And the canoe slid away from me. My nails dug into the wood of the pier.

"Help!" I yelled, hugging the dock.

One minute I was stretched between the dock and the canoe.

The next, the canoe floated away, leaving my feet dangling over the gurgling, smelly, mucky *poisoned* water.

My feet weren't touching the water. But I figured the fumes alone were lethal.

Any minute now my toes were probably going to fall off and plop into the water.

Kids Outsmart Dogs, Guards and Selves

"GOTCHA!"

Two strong hands caught me beneath the arms. A guard pulled me onto the dock.

Looking down, I noticed I still had all my toes. They weren't even rotting.

Looking up, I saw the close-shaved hair and ice-cold eyes of a guard. "Kids!" he said, as if he were saying "Snakes!"

Gary regained control of the canoe and paddled back. He jumped onto the dock and tied up the canoe.

"Let her go," he shouted.

To be honest, I was impressed by the way Gary swung into action. I guess all that testosterone can come in handy.

Gary grabbed the arm of a guard—the bigger one. "You've no right—"

"Oh, yes, I do," said the guard. "You kids are trespassing on private property and that, as you brats well know, is against the law. Let's go."

"How about if we just paddle back to where we came from?" I suggested with a sugary smile that would have done Megan proud.

The hefty guard just said, "You two are coming with us."

So that's how Gary and I got the grand tour of the security office at Riverhead Paper. Stuck in our metal chairs, we waited for the head guy to show up. I didn't have my journal, so I borrowed a paper and pen from one of the guards and started writing:

A metal desk. Filing cabinets. Concrete floor. Metal chairs. Coffeepot that looks murkier than the river. Not a single thing on the walls.

Talk about dreary. It makes the rest of the mill look like a theme park.

I paused. One guard was reading over my shoulder.

"Do you mind?" I folded up the paper.

He just shook his head as the main security

guy strolled in. A barrel-chested man with thick black hair, he did not smile.

Actually, nobody was smiling.

"What were you two doing out there?" asked the chief.

"Well, sir," Gary began. "We were just out for a canoe ride when the current took us off course. We tried to paddle out, but . . ."

I tuned him out. The image of my litmus strip swirling away in the river still haunted me. I'd gotten proof, and I'd let it slip through my fingers. Literally. Now I knew my story was accurate, but I'd botched up the chance to prove it.

"I can't believe we got caught," I said from the seat of the Jeep a half hour later.

Gram had come to the mill to pick me up. Gary had called his brother, who showed up to vouch for Gary and the canoe. Even though the guards had acted like we were going to jail, Gary had softened them up. They'd actually fallen for the lie about the wind pushing our canoe.

That's Gary—full of wind. But today his ability to blow smoke up someone's shorts had come in handy.

"Sounds like the time I tried to get a quote from President Nixon about the Watergate break-in," Gram said when I confessed the whole story during the drive home. "The Secret Service found me waiting behind a bush in the White House Rose Garden. They didn't let me paddle away, either."

The thought of my grandmother crouching in one of her power suits was funny. But I wasn't smiling. Neither was Gram. "They wanted to take away my press pass," she added.

"I get the message," I told her. "But what else could I do? I mean, three months of chemical emissions figures are missing! I knew the acid test would be quick and simple. I had to do it."

"So you break into the mill?" Gram probed. "You trespass? You take a canoe out without telling—"

"I know, I know. But *missing paperwork*! I knew they were trying to cover up something. And I was right."

"Really?" Gram stole a glance at me, then turned back to the road. "So you've got the facts to back up your story."

"Had the facts." I flopped back against the car seat and filled her in about the acid test. "I dropped the litmus strip into the river."

"Oh, Casey," Gram said sympathetically. "What a bummer. Totally." She hesitated. "And I'm afraid there's more bad news for your story. There's a message on the voice mail for you. From Project Green."

"Dr. Dawn!" I bolted up. "She finally called back? Great! Maybe I she has the facts I need."

She handed me the cell phone. "Go on. Retrieve the message."

I punched in the numbers and code to get our answering machine. A woman's voice started:

"This is Dr. Dawn Forrest—from Project Green. I'm sorry we keep missing each other. Anyway—I'm headed out of town for a conference. I'll be back in two weeks."

"No, no!" I groaned. "You can't go yet!" I needed her help.

"They told me you were interested in . . . let's see . . . the Sussex River tests? There's a bit of misinformation out there. Keep in mind that none of our test results are published yet. And they shouldn't be."

"What?" I couldn't believe what I was hearing.

Frowning, Gram kept her eyes on the road.

"Something got posted prematurely on our web site—I don't know how. Sometimes our volunteers find it hard to separate fact and suspicion. We *are* conducting a test of the water purity. When so many dead fish turn up on the shoreline, we want to know why. But sometimes wildlife die from natural causes. And so far we do not have conclusive readings on dioxins or any other toxic chemicals in the river."

"What?" I cringed. So all the Project Green references in my story were . . . *wrong*?

"We'll send you the study when it's complete," Dr. Dawn went on. "In a few months. Thanks, Casey. Okay, 'bye."

I saved the message and turned off the phone.

"That stinks," I muttered. I told Gram what Dr. Dawn had said.

Gram nodded. "What's your next step?"

I sank back into the seat as the dark night streaked by. "Retirement," I muttered. "My journalism career is over. I am up the river without a paddle. Without a boogie board. Without a beach ball."

Gram maneuvered the Jeep around a curve. "You've got a reporter's instincts, Casey. And a good reporter always has another angle. A different way to approach someone . . . or something."

It was nice to know my grandmother had faith in me.

Personally, I was beginning to wonder.

CHAPTER 18

Sugarplum Fairy Declares War

THAT NIGHT MY bedroom was the newsroom once again. Fingers clacking on keyboard, I went over everything I knew about Riverhead and the Sussex. I needed a new angle to crack the story. If there was one.

After brainstorming with Griffin through e-mail, I made a list in my journal:

WEDNESDAY NIGHT

1. Call Tyler's dad directly. Maybe he'll talk? Maybe he wants to blow the whistle on the mill?

2. Call Project Green—MUST REACH

DR. DAWN—CAN E-MAIL HER ANYWHERE
IN THE WORLD!!!
3. Disguise self as Girl Scout and go
back to plant with cookies. Everybody
loves cookies.
4. Interview fish from Sussex. Do story
through eyes of a fish.

By ten thirty that night, I had to cross off all four of the items.

Tyler's father, Mr. McKenzie, wasn't going to talk to me. I'd gotten as close as his wife, who'd called me "that Casey girl" before telling me to get lost. Apparently "that Tyler boy" had warned his parents about me.

After some pushing, the woman at Project Green had given me Dr. Dawn's pager number. But she also mentioned that the scientist was in transit tonight. Tomorrow morning she would be running a seminar. I had a chance—a *chance*—of reaching her in the afternoon.

The mill seemed like the most likely place to get more incriminating information. But at this point I knew I was not welcome there, even if I disguised myself as a *cookie*.

As for interviewing the fish? Okay, it was past my 10 P.M. lights out and I was tired. Don't blame me for getting punchy. Besides, the fish I needed to talk to were dead.

I guess you'd understand why I wasn't in the best of moods when I walked into the *Real News* office Thursday morning. Megan and Ringo were chained to computers. Toni sat at Dalmatian Station, cutting around the edges of photos.

"Casey." Megan pushed back her bangs. No barrettes today. Just blond hair tucked behind her ears. "Do you have final copy for us?"

"Soon," I lied, slipping off my backpack. Why worry Megan? I still had time.

"I got it!" Ringo called from behind a PC. "It's fixed."

Glancing over at his screen, I saw the menu for Disktop, the desktop publishing program.

"We can load in stories to format," Ringo announced proudly.

"Super!" Megan nodded. "You can start with these stories," she said, handing Ringo a disk. "We have a few more to edit."

"And that's it?" Toni asked. "We're done?"

Ringo shook his head. "Then we've got to lay out each page."

"Figure out which photographs should go where," I added. "Write captions."

"Decide on graphics and borders," Megan said.

Toni sank into a chair. "Lame-o. We'll be here all night. And I've got to baby-sit. This is too much work."

Megan and I exchanged a look of concern.

"Don't say that," Megan said. She grabbed a stack of papers and headed out. "I want to get these copied for Mr. Baxter. Be right back."

The tone in the newsroom was still tentative.

"We can do it," I said. "Layout is easy. Piece of cake." I checked my watch. Two minutes till our meeting with Mr. Baxter. "Too bad we have to waste time in classes!"

"You're telling me," Toni said, grabbing her portfolio. She unzipped it and pulled out a few photos. "Casey, here."

I groaned when I saw the photographs of the newly renovated cafeteria. Gleaming floors. Shiny aluminum kitchen equipment. Deluxe salad bar.

It was as newsworthy as the dust balls underneath my bed at home.

Then another photograph caught my eye. I did a double take. Two figures in a canoe?

"Hey . . . this is Gary and me!"

Quickly, I flipped through the three photos that were stacked underneath. One showed me dipping the test strip into the Sussex River. The mill pipes were gaping monsters in the background.

The second was a shot of the guard pulling me up onto the dock while the German shepherds strained against their leashes.

The final photo showed the guards escorting Gary and me to the mill.

Primo action shots, every one.

I gaped at Toni. "Coolness. But how . . . ?"

"Telephoto lens," she supplied. "I was on the opposite bank. I rode my bike over after Gary paged me with the tip."

"But . . . why?" I asked.

She planted her hands on the hips of her baggy jeans. Her amber eyes were sharp, penetrating. "Maybe you go crazy to get a story, Casey. And maybe you have, like, a lot of opinions that nobody wants to hear—"

"What?" I exclaimed.

"But you also have a lot of nerve. I like nerve," Toni went on. "I figure if a miracle happens and you get your story, I am going to make sure there are photos to go with it. Spectacular photos."

She actually smiled at me.

And I actually smiled back. "Thanks a lot." It felt good to know that Toni was behind me.

Megan returned with an armload of photocopies. "More shots for this edition?" she asked cheerfully. She glanced at the shots, and suddenly she wasn't so perky. "What—?" Plucking the photos from my hands, she stared in horror. "What were you guys doing? Canoeing by the mill? If that area is polluted, you could have fallen in and . . . Are you crazy?"

Just then Gary came in, his big, chunky sneakers nearly bouncing on the floor. "Hey, guys. Casey filled you in on our adventure?"

"Adventure?" Megan gaped at Gary. "No, Gary. An adventure is a roller coaster ride. A ski trip. This is total brain failure. How could you guys be so stupid?"

"Gary helped me research a story," I said defensively.

"Didn't we talk about this after your last problem at the mill?" Megan's eyes shifted to the second photo. "Police?" She winced. "*Police!* Were you arrested?"

"Actually, they're security guards," Gary boasted. "They talked a good game. Right, Casey? Did you really think they were going to put us in jail?"

"Not for a minute," I said. "Though they did have us on trespassing."

"Only because I was trying to steady the canoe," Gary said. "To keep Casey from falling into the river."

"Falling in?" Megan's perfect complexion was now stained with pink. "Do you know how sick you could have gotten if—"

"But I didn't," I said. "We're fine. *And* I got the information I wanted. Well, I don't have it anymore. But I—"

Just then Mr. Baxter shuffled in and dumped his coat and briefcase onto the table. "Sorry I'm late."

"Mr. Baxter." Megan turned and handed him the photos. "Did you know about this?"

"No." He eyed Gary and me curiously. "What's the deal here?"

Bursting with pride, Gary gave everyone a play-by-play recap. With windspeed, swirling currents and something about being in the zone. He made it sound like I was bungee-jumping from the dock.

Mr. Baxter listened cautiously. Ringo and Toni were amused. Megan looked like she was going to faint on the floor.

"We have to think about the newspaper's reputation. Ever heard of responsible journalism? We can't take chances," Megan said, folding her arms. "I cannot work with someone who takes foolish risks."

From the way she glared at me, I knew that "someone" was me. Funny how Gary could walk away from this looking like a star, while Megan made me out to be a daredevil.

"Excuse me if I go after a *real* news story," I said. "From now on I'll just sit around and write cute ditties about the human pyramid the cheerleaders made last week. Or whether we should go with a tropical paradise theme for the school dance. Is that what you want to hear?"

Megan waved the river photos at me. "I want to hear you promise you won't take any more foolish chances."

"Never," I snapped. "I will never make that promise."

"People," Mr. Baxter interrupted. "Let's calm down."

"A *real* reporter has to be willing to take risks," I shot back at Megan. "For your information, I got a very important lead from that canoe trip."

"Are you trying to say that I'm *not* a real reporter?" Angry red spots rose to Megan's cheeks.

"Girls, please. . . ." Mr. Baxter held up a hand.

But I wasn't finished making my case.

"Megan doesn't care about the news, Mr. Baxter," I said. "Can't you see that she's holding me back? She's a rope around my neck. A leash! I'm talking issues, and she's worried about making sure no one looks bad! She's . . . she's . . . shallow!"

While I spoke, Megan's face got redder and redder. Finally she jumped up, her hands balled into fists. "Stop it! Just stop—right now!" she screamed.

Everyone stared at her in total shock.

"You think *I'm* holding *you* back?" Megan scowled at me. "Do you think it's easy to put together an entire newspaper with you criticizing every single suggestion? Everything I do, you make fun of or sneer at. Just because I'm not covering a war or a tornado, that doesn't give you the right to put me down."

I swallowed as Megan took a breath, then raged on.

"So what if I like to get involved with school events? So what if I like to make a good impression? That doesn't mean I'm shallow," she said. "I'm not! And I care about the kids at this school. Which you obviously do not. This isn't *The New York Times*. And it isn't *The Casey Smith Paper*, either. This is *our* paper. It belongs to all of us. So we can all have a voice and our voices can be heard! That's the point. At least that's what I thought we were doing here. And I've been working really hard on *Real News*. The least you could do is show some appreciation for that." Megan gulped, like she was trying to stop. But she couldn't. It was like a dam had burst.

"You mock me all the time and, yeah, you're funny when you do it and people laugh—I know you call me the Sugarplum Fairy—but that stuff hurts, Casey. It's mean. Besides, if you've got something nasty to say about me, why don't you have the guts to say it to my face? You think I'm shallow? Well, I say you're a coward. A big, fat, condescending, egotistical coward. What do you think about that?"

She stopped and dropped into a chair. The room was silent.

Everyone looked at me as if they expected an answer. And normally I would have had a cutting comeback up my sleeve. But I was so surprised to see Megan's explosion that, for a second, words escaped me.

I, Casey Smith, was speechless.

CHAPTER 19

Reporter Wins Pulitzer for Ham Sandwich Exposé

For a long moment no one said anything.

Finally Mr. Baxter sighed. "Maybe this whole notion of a student paper should end," he said.

"What are you saying, Mr. B.?" asked Gary.

Mr. Baxter shifted in his chair, looking uncomfortable. "You're behind schedule. You're tearing each other down. You have to ask yourself if your priorities are in the right place."

Yes, I wanted to shout. But I didn't. I wasn't sure anything I had to say would be welcome right now.

"Maybe we should delay publication," he said.

No!

"Do the students really need a paper every week?" Mr. Baxter went on.

Yes. But no one spoke. We were shell-shocked by Megan's explosion.

Mr. Baxter frowned. "With all your schoolwork and other activities, maybe these deadlines are too tight."

"Journalists work on deadline," I said.

"But this paper is only going to get published if you work together." Mr. Baxter looked pointedly at Megan and me. "It's not the Casey paper. Or the Megan paper. And I'm not here to mediate. If you kids can't work out your differences, you will no longer have me as a faculty advisor."

No advisor meant no newspaper.

And that was not something I was willing to consider. Something snapped inside me. The paper was more important than Megan or me. Whatever our problems, they could wait. The paper couldn't.

"We'll do it," I said quickly. "We'll work together. We'll help each other, right, Megan?" I turned to her.

"What?" Megan blinked like someone waking from a magician's spell.

The homeroom bell rang. Outside, people scrambled down the hall.

"Well, I'm not convinced," said Mr. Baxter. "We didn't even get to the stories in this week's edition. And you need to work out your layout today." He took a clipped stack of papers from his briefcase and put them on the spotted table. "But if you kids can do it, I'll stick in there for now. My notes are in the margins. What's going on the front page?"

"'MILL POLLUTING THE SUSSEX,'" I blurted out.

"'CAFETERIA RENOVATED!'" Megan insisted.

With a last glance at Megan and me, he said, "Work it out." Then he left the office.

Ringo, Toni and Gary grabbed their stuff and followed him out, anxious to escape the battle scene.

That left Megan and me.

"The cafeteria story?" she said, holding out one hand. "I need it."

"I'm still polishing," I lied.

"You can give it to me at lunchtime," she said, turning away. She grabbed her backpack and left the gray gloom room without turning back. Was she mad? Embarrassed? Relieved that I had jumped in to make peace? Or sorry the whole paper hadn't been junked?

The only thing I knew for sure was that I was way behind on two story assignments, and we still had no front page.

I was going to be late for homeroom. But if I could just jot down a few sentences, I would feel better. I turned to PC and punched in my title:

Renovated Cafeteria Gets a New
Lease on Life, Liver and the
Pursuit of Ham Sandwiches

I stared at the words. Then I groaned.
"I have definitely reached a new low."

All morning I couldn't get Megan out of my mind. The way she'd yelled. The things she'd said about me.

Ouch. Some of them were true.

We were different, Megan and I. We always would be. Megan's desire for neat and easy stories wasn't going to change my approach. I had paddled up a smelly river for a story, and I would do it again.

On the other hand, Megan did have a point about being responsible. My feature on Riverhead Paper was not ready to publish. Without proof it was too thin. Irresponsible journalism. I knew there was a story there, but the bottom line? I was out of time.

Time to admit defeat and whip up the cafeteria story. But it's hard to get inspired by visions of speckled floor tile and aluminum sinks dancing in your head. My only break was that my science teacher, Ms. Strader, was out sick. The substitute took us to the library to do some lame assignment that I finished in thirty seconds. That left the entire period to work on a PC there.

I even managed to slip out to the cafeteria and get a few quotes from the people who doled out food. Then, digging around in the admin office, I finagled a copy of the architect's plans.

Sound interesting? It wasn't. And five months or five years from now, no one would remember it or care.

That's the difference between a news story and a fluff piece. A news story grabs you and shakes you up. A fluff piece—well, it will lull you to sleep.

By lunchtime, I had a draft for Megan. The air in the newsroom was light and friendly. The calm after the storm.

I handed my story to Megan and checked my watch. Was it too early to page Dr. Dawn? And what if the mill story broke? Was there still time to get it into this week's edition?

I glanced around. Pencil in hand, Megan began to edit my cafeteria piece. Gary and Toni brainstormed captions for baseball photos.

"'Miller at the plate,'" Toni suggested.

"No!" Gary insisted. "'Miller slides into the plate!'"

Ringo was trying to cut down a story to fit on page three. "I'm stuck," he told me, staring at the formatted story on the screen. "Casey, help."

"How about taking out this sentence?" I suggested. Sliding onto the edge of his desk, I accidentally knocked his red spiral notebook to the floor. Papers and napkins and odd scraps slipped out. They all had doodles on them.

I bent down and picked up the doodles. Actually, they were more like cartoons now.

"Hey," I said. "Your drawings are getting better."

Ringo shrugged. "You think so?"

"Definitely! They're so weird," I said, laughing at them. "I mean good weird. Not weird weird. But who is this kid you keep drawing?"

Ringo looked over my shoulder. "That's Simon. He's my main man."

As I sifted through the pages, Simon went through the routine at Trumbull.

Simon at the orientation assembly. Simon in the cafeteria. Simon at the Hole-in-the-Mall. Simon trying to figure out the computer catalog in the library.

"Why didn't you tell me you were such a great cartoonist?" I asked.

Ringo shrugged. "You didn't ask."

I paused. He was right.

SIMON SAYS!

The middle isn't a terrible place to be... It's like the cream in a twinkie... the stuffing in a turkey... the jelly in a doughnut... the jam between your toes

Tomato—sliced or cherry?
Carrots—whole or grated?
Lettuce—iceberg or romaine?
Sprouts—bean or alfalfa?
I'll have a burger with ketchup.
from a Bottle... please

I hadn't really paid much attention. I shook out the napkin I'd seen Ringo draw on while we were at the Hole-in-the-Mall.

"Simon. . . . How did you think him up?"

Ringo shrugged. "Actually, he kind of thought himself into my brain," he told me. "I just drew him one day."

"Simon is great," I said. "You could really—" I stopped in mid-sentence, staring at the cartoons. "Wait! This is perfect! It's exactly what we need!"

"It is?" Ringo turned away from the keyboard. "Who's we?"

"Everyone at Trumbull Middle School!" I told

him. "Don't you see? 'Simon' is a total reflection of what goes on here. Everyone can relate to him."

He squinted. "Do you think so?"

I turned to the other staffers. "You've got to look at this stuff."

They stopped what they were doing and joined us.

"It reminds me of the comic strips in real newspapers," Gary said.

"Very good," Toni agreed. "But where's the girl character?"

Ringo frowned. "She hasn't popped into my head yet."

Megan gushed over the drawings. "This is exactly what *Real News* needs to give it a totally original feel. We can squeeze a few cartoons in this issue. If you want us to, that is."

Ringo frowned. "Serious?"

"Absolutely," I told him.

"Cool." Ringo grinned. "I mean, I really wanted to add something to the paper. This is way cool."

Megan shook her head as she went back to her desk. "You know, Ringo, you didn't need Simon to be part of the team. You've been a huge help with our layout."

"I have?" Ringo asked. He was actually turning red.

"Easy, Megan," I warned, picking up the scraps of paper still on the floor. "You don't want him to suffer from compliment overload."

"That's okay," Ringo said. "I can take it."

I looked at a loose sheet of paper showing Simon visiting a local plant. Ringo hadn't given the place a name, but I recognized the fenced-in metal buildings of Riverhead Paper.

"This one needs a caption," I said. As I handed it back to Ringo, I noticed print on the reverse side.

"You drew this on the back of a memo," I said.

"Reduce, reuse, and recycle." Ringo grinned. "I got that from the recycle bin at the mill. Remember when we were hanging out by the copy machine?"

I snatched it away from him. "A Riverhead Paper memo!"

The print leaped out at me.

"I don't think this is scrap, Ringo. It's been signed by the supervisor of the water-treatment facility. And look at this!"

I jabbed my finger at the word *CONFIDENTIAL*, which was spelled out on top in capital letters. Beneath was the text of the memo:

```
    Emissions figures from the past
  three months (copies attached)
```

```
suggest a malfunction in our
water-treatment facility. This
is a critical situation, which
necessitates quick and quiet
action. Please advise.
```

Short. But revealing.

"Do you know what this means?" I faced Ringo.

"That the supervisor likes to use big words?" Ringo said, staring at the memo.

"It means that I was right!" I crowed. "No wonder I couldn't find the emissions figures for the past three months! The supervisor hid them because they showed that the water-treatment facility wasn't working!"

Megan and Gary and Toni stopped what they were doing and crowded around.

"Is this for real?" Toni asked.

"Not only that," I said, "it sounds like he wants to sweep the whole thing under the rug. I mean, why else would he say he wants to take care of it quietly?"

I was talking and flipping through the loose scraps of paper at the same time. "Riverhead Paper has probably been polluting big-time! But I need to see those figures. . . ." I began turning over other cartoons, frantically searching for more memos.

"Charts!" I stood up and gripped Ringo's shoulders. "I need charts! Did you get copies of the charts?"

"Whoa!" Megan said. "Don't kill the messenger."

"Ringo, think hard. Did you do any other drawings at the mill?" I demanded.

Ringo bit his lower lip. "Wait a minute! I started one of Bud-the-dog. But I didn't finish it."

"Find it!" Frantically, I handed him the pile of paper.

He flipped through it quickly. "It's not in there," he said.

"Where, then?" I demanded. "In your shoe? In the jeans you wore that day?"

Ringo shook his head and patted the pocket of his denim shirt. "It was in here."

I held my breath as he reached into the pocket, fishing around.

It was empty.

"I guess it fell out," Ringo said apologetically.

The energy seemed to rush out of the room, like a deflating balloon. I slumped down in a chair and stared at the floor. Again, I'd come so close. . . .

My eyes wandered to Dalmatian Station. I realized that ugly table was growing on me, from the spotted surface to the wobbly lime-green leg braced by a wad of paper.

A wad of paper.

"Wait!" I shouted.

I vaguely remembered seeing Ringo stick paper under the table leg to stop the table from tilting. And he had taken it out of his pocket.

Could it be?

Diving to my knees, I lifted a table leg and pulled out the folded paper under it.

"This is it!" I shouted. "A memo! From the executive vice president to the supervisor:

```
   It is regrettable, but the
malfunction in our water-treatment
facility has resulted in chemical
emissions exceeding legal limits . . .
```

The memo included columns of numbers—emissions figures. The numbers didn't mean much to me. But the memo was proof, spelled out in cold, hard print, that Riverhead Paper was breaking the law.

And that was all I needed.

CHAPTER 20

Dirty, Rotten Meanies at Mill Hung Out to Dry

"THIS IS IT!" I smoothed my hands over the rumpled paper. "This is the proof I need."

Megan shook her head. "I can't believe it."

"I got it!" I jumped up and waved the paper. Megan was actually smiling as I skipped over to a PC. "My story will need some changes. Maybe I should move the part about Riverhead Paper to the beginning."

"Hold on a second," Gary said. "You can't run that in this issue. It's too late."

"I'll make it," I insisted. I slid my disk into the computer and brought up my pollution story.

"Casey, page one is ready to go," Toni pointed out. "There's no time."

"Are you kidding me?" I turned back to study their faces. "This is news. *Real* news that kids need to know. Are you going to help me get this into shape?"

No one moved.

"Or are you just going to stand there and pretend that the story of our cafeteria is going to blow kids out of the water?"

Megan checked her watch and sighed. "Lunch is over in twenty minutes."

I couldn't believe it. How could they let a story like this fall through the cracks? Just because of a deadline?

Then, suddenly, Megan was talking. "We'll have to work super fast." She turned to the others. "Toni, you have a good eye. Go through Ringo's Simon cartoons and see what might work in this issue."

Toni picked up Ringo's notebook and started spreading his drawings out on the table.

"Gary," Megan continued, "finish off those picture captions. The sports page is almost finished. Ringo, keep going with the page two format. And you—"

She came over and wheeled my chair back toward the computer. "Back to that rewrite. We have a late-breaking story to publish."

Excitement sparked inside me as I looked back at the glowing monitor. Now *this* was journalism. But before I could begin, there was one thing

I had to do. I turned back to Megan. There she was in all her pink preppiness. A pink jumper today. With tiny rosebuds on the collar. She could have sunk my story. Given the friction between us, I'd expected her to sink the story. But she didn't.

"Thanks," I said.

"Ha!" She walked briskly back to her desk. "Don't thank me yet. We're not even half finished!"

Okay, she was a priss and a prude. But the girl had class.

The rest of Thursday was a blur of editorial madness. The final bell sent us running back to the *Real News* office to work after school in order to finish.

I paged Dr. Dawn and she called back on Mr. Baxter's classroom line. When I told her what I'd found, she wanted to see the numbers. So Mr. Baxter helped me fax them to her hotel from the school office.

After that, facts rolled into place like . . . like paper on a giant reel.

"These are devastating levels of toxins," Dr. Dawn told me when she called back. "Five times the level of legal limits. And you have proof that Riverhead *knows* they're breaking the law and that they're releasing false data."

"It's a cover-up," I said.

"Exactly," she said. "Once this is reported, Riverhead is going to be shut down. This pollution will be stopped. Thanks to you, Casey."

Still reeling with excitement, I got a few quotes from Dr. Dawn, then rushed back to the newspaper office. The Riverhead story had taken on a life of its own. Now it wasn't just about pollution. It was about a cover-up. A company that broke the law. A company that lied to a community. And by lying, they'd put our community at risk.

As I reworked my story, the other kids worked on the layout. They input changes. They spell-checked. They cut and added words to make things fit. They cropped photos and laughed at Ringo's cartoons.

We called home to get permission to stay late. Mr. Baxter agreed to stick around so we could keep the office open. He spent most of the time grading essays in the faculty lounge. But now and then he poked his head in and answered questions.

We worked through dinner. Around six Gary had to leave to study for a science test. Toni's father came to pick her up at six thirty. And Ringo hitched a ride with them, since he had a seven-o'clock curfew.

Suddenly, it was just Megan and me.

We had input my Riverhead story, but the front page was really tight. With the pollution story, two of Toni's photos and the beginning of the story on the cafeteria, the page was over-crowded.

"It's not working." I frowned at the screen. "We have to trim the pollution story. Maybe cut it in half."

"But how?" Megan's face glowed blue from the monitor. "There's no padding in the story. No throw-away lines. And Toni's photos grab your attention."

I sighed. It was getting late. And we were stuck.

"Let's try this." Megan hit a few keys and . . . POOF!

The front page was reformatted—

Minus the cafeteria story.

"Wait." I blinked. "Are you sure?"

"We can squeeze the cafeteria piece on to page two. Or page five. But it's going to take some work. More reformatting." Megan checked her watch.

"Maybe we can do a teaser for the cafeteria story on page one," I heard myself saying. Sheesh! I was getting soft. But it wasn't a bad story. And I wanted to be a team player. Besides, that meant I got my byline on the front page twice.

"Super idea." Megan beamed. "It's going to take some time, though."

This time, I checked her watch.

"It's seven thirty."

"Are you up for it?" she asked.

I stretched my arms out. "I'll stay all night!"

"You may have to," Megan said as her fingers flew over the keyboard. "I hope Mr. Baxter doesn't mind."

Just after eight Mr. Baxter appeared in the doorway. "I don't know about you, but I'm ready to turn into a pumpkin."

"We're just printing out a layout," I said, feeling a sense of accomplishment.

Megan yawned. "We can insert the photos and art in the morning."

When Mr. Baxter left to call Gram and ask her to pick us up, Megan and I straightened up.

I stacked the sheets on the table at Dalmatian Station, making sure the edges were all lined up. Somehow I didn't want to leave them behind.

What if there was a fire in the school? An earthquake? What if a sinkhole formed and swallowed up our layout and all our computer data overnight? What if a big bear came through the window and . . .

"I know," Megan said, coming up next to me. "You don't want to leave it behind."

I nodded. "We did it."

Her eyes flashed with warmth as she lifted her chin. "Yup. And we're going to do it again next week. And the week after. And the week after that."

"That's the great part about the news," I said, grabbing my backpack. "It just keeps on happening."

"Don't remind me," she said. She yawned again as she followed me out the door. "Are you sure your grandmother doesn't mind dropping me off?"

"No problem." I reached back to flip off the lights. "And on the way, we can talk about front-page stories for next week's edition."

Front-Page Story Mushrooms
Like Atomic Bomb

DATELINE: MONDAY MORNING

It's in lockers. Propped up at lunch tables. Kids carry it under their arms and bury their noses in it between classes.

"It" is <u>Real News</u>, the new voice of kids at Trumbull Middle School.

"Casey."

I had blocked out the noise of the cafeteria, where kids were loud as usual. But at least today they were loud about *Real News*, which had been distributed in homerooms across the school that morning.

"Casey." Ringo nudged my arm.

Glancing up from my journal, I took the napkin he handed me. It was a sketch of Simon—with a dog. Simon was telling the dog:

OKAY. You go to school. I'll watch the factory.

I smiled. "Maybe you should write an editorial about the life of a guard dog."

Just then Toni came over and flashed a copy of *Real News* in front of us.

"Do these photos look fantastic, or what?" she said, sliding onto the bench beside Ringo.

"Fantastic," I agreed. For the gazillionth time, I soaked up the front-page headline:

RIVERHEAD PAPER POLLUTING LOCAL WATERS

There, right under the headline, was my name.

Casey Smith

In black and white.

Every time I looked at it, I felt a thrill. I knew I always would.

"And you guys thought it couldn't be done," I said, grinning.

Glancing up, I saw Megan and Gary reading over my shoulder.

"But we did it," Megan said.

"I still don't get it," Gary said. "Why is a story about a paper mill more important than a profile of a basketball superstar? A guy who'll probably go pro."

"In, like, a hundred years," Toni pointed out.

Ringo shrugged, fingering the edge of the newspaper. "I'm still worried about Bud-the-dog."

"Your profile is great, Gary," Megan put in. "And people love Simon—and the photos. The thing is, it all came together."

Copies of *Real News* were open at every table. It was a hit.

And Megan was right. The paper existed because we had worked together. Sharing ideas. Sharing grunt work.

"We hit the right combination," I said. And I really believed it. "This issue has a solid news story. Sports. Some back-to-school stuff. Cartoons."

"Exactly." Megan adjusted her red-satin headband. "Kids want to be entertained. But it's also important to know about what's happening around us."

Hearing that, I grinned. Maybe there was hope for Megan after all.

As Toni flipped the pages I stopped her. There was one story I hadn't read through. Megan's piece on school activities, which was edited by Gary.

JUST DO IT!
TRUMBULL'S ACTIVITIES OFFER
SOMETHING FOR EVERYONE
By Megan O'Connor

I'd skipped it because I had zero interest in the subject. But now I was curious. As I read, I realized Megan had quoted what I had said about Yearbook:

Sure, some people say that
Yearbook is just a social club for
airheads. But how can you know
for sure if you don't give it a
chance?

The Crafts Club has a reputation
for being a "hobby." But last year,
Chloe Pettit's sculpture entitled
"Star Dancer" won first place at
the state art competition. Chloe
came away with a $500 prize and
a scholarship to art school.
Her "hobby" may well become a
vocation.

Look beyond the stereotypes. Try
out different clubs and activities.
Decide for yourself. What is each
group about? And which one is
right for you?

I hated to admit it, but her story was insightful. Concise. Relevant. But I didn't want her to get cocky.

"Just what we need," I grumbled. "A zillion kids joining the debate team, Yearbook, intramurals *and* the sixth-grade bake-off."

"I missed a bake-off?" Ringo's gray eyes flashed with alarm. "Why didn't anyone tell me?"

"She's joking," Megan said.

"I'm joking," I said at the same time.

We glanced at each other. A team.

Just then someone slapped a copy of *Real News* onto the lunch table in front of me. It was Tyler—and he didn't look happy.

"Congratulations, Casey," he said flatly.

"On what?" I asked, not sure I wanted to know.

"Some environmental action group got a copy of your story," he went on.

That would be Project Green, I thought. I had e-mailed a copy of the story to Dr. Dawn on Friday. I'd also sent it to Griffin. Ms. Dombrowski *The New York Times*. The local newspaper. And my parents in Asia.

"This group . . ." Tyler went on, his eyes sharp with anger. "They're mobilizing against Riverhead Paper. They're going for a court order. There's going to be an official investigation."

He shook his head, looking miserable. "They're going to close down the mill."

"That's weird." Ringo stopped doodling for a moment. "The paper just came out this morning. I guess word travels fast in the computer age."

I wanted to kick him under the table, but he was too far away.

"It's not so bad," Megan told Tyler. "So they close down the mill until the water-treatment system is repaired. Things will be better when they reopen. Maybe they'll even improve the system, right?"

He just stared off, a glum expression on his face.

"No more Bald Hill," I said encouragingly. "No more awful smell."

"No more jobs," he muttered.

"What? What do you mean 'no more jobs'?"

Tyler's brown eyes blazed with fury. "My father's going to be laid off," he told me. "And he's not the only one. Do you know how many people will lose their jobs when that mill closes?"

"But they can go back after the repairs are finished," I told him. "Right?"

He shrugged. "Maybe. Maybe not. The government will fine Riverhead. That will cost the company a lot of money. Repairing whatever went wrong will cost the company a lot of money. And they'll lose money while they're closed. In the end, they may not be able to hire everyone back. *If* they reopen at all. Besides, people could go to jail if they can prove there was a cover-up. People who just did what their bosses told them to do. People like my father."

I had been floating all morning. Now, looking at Tyler, I felt as if someone had poked a hole in me and let the air out.

I wanted to say something—but what?

"My father's going to be out of a job." Tyler's eyes were ice cold. "All because of you."

"But, Tyler," I said, with all the dignity I could muster, "we were just doing the right thing."

"Really. And who made you the judge of right and wrong, Casey?"

Poison-Pen Letter Stains Journalist's Career

EVERYONE WAS SILENT as Tyler walked away through the crowd at the cafeteria door.

"I feel terrible," Megan said.

Gary shook his head. "I can't believe our six-page middle-school paper could do that. I mean, no one can really blame us. Can they? We're not responsible."

Gary's words jolted me into action. I jumped up and I ran out the cafeteria door.

"Tyler, wait!" I called.

He was already halfway down the hall.

I fell into step beside him, talking fast.

"Riverhead Paper was polluting. They were breaking the law," I said, breathlessly. "And their silence endangered the health of anyone who went near that river. I just wanted to stop it. I never meant for anyone to get laid off."

"Then I guess none of us got what we wanted. Thanks, Casey." His sarcasm hurt me. "Thanks a lot."

"Tyler, I wrote the story to make people aware of a dangerous situation. I wanted to fix a problem. Make things better—not worse."

"Well, things are worse," he said, stopping in front of his locker. "At least, they will be for me. Especially if we have to leave Abbington."

"Leave Abbington? Why?"

He shrugged. "You know anyone in Abbington who wants to hire a chemical engineer?"

"That's a hypothetical question, right?"

Tyler opened his locker and exchanged books.

"Look, maybe things will work out in the end," I told him. I knew it sounded lame. But what could I say? "It will be a good thing in the long run. Anything that cuts down on pollution is. Really."

Tyler slammed the door of his locker. "Go ahead and believe that if you want. Anyway, this is for you."

I hadn't even noticed the envelope in Tyler's right hand. He handed it to me, in a cool gesture.

Suddenly, I felt really far away from him.

Not a friend. An enemy.

That's what he thought of me now.

"It's for the next edition of *Real News*," he said. Then he walked away.

Feeling hurt and disappointed, I took the envelope and wandered back to the newspaper office. Alone in the room, I opened it and started reading:

To the Editor:

Casey Smith's article on Riverhead Paper only gives one side of the story. Casey says that no amount of pollution is acceptable. But now several hundred people at Riverhead Paper risk losing their jobs.

Casey seems to care a lot about the planet. But what about the people who live here? Should people lose their jobs just because a machine malfunctions?

People need paper, and people need jobs. If Riverhead Paper closes, we will lose an important source of both of those things.

Casey Smith is only reporting one side of this story. She needs to realize that people rely on this company for jobs and paper. She also needs to consider the consequences of the articles she writes. A voice is a powerful thing to have.

Sincerely,
Tyler McKenzie

"Casey?" Megan stood in the doorway, her face tentative. She wasn't sure whether or not to come in.

"He wrote a letter to the editor. He's attacking my story." I pushed the sheet toward her. "I had the facts. Riverhead Paper was breaking the law and covering it up. Pollution! And that's wrong. End of story. The truth is on my side!"

I rubbed my eyes. "So why do I feel so awful?"

Megan had been reading over Tyler's letter while I spoke. Now she said, "We have to publish this."

"Why?" I cried. "He's being so unfair!"

Megan bit her lip. "We agreed that the whole purpose of *Real News* is to give kids a voice. That means all kids, not just us."

I crossed my arms on the desk and let my head fall onto them. "I keep thinking about what Tyler said—that people losing their jobs is a high price to pay for saving the environment."

"He does have a point," Megan said, sitting down next to me. "But so do you. Pollution *is* wrong. Sometimes I wish I had the guts to speak out the way you do. I just hate to hurt people's feelings."

"It's who you are," I told her. "You're a good person, Megan. I'm not sure I am."

Megan's eyes softened. "That's not true. You

mean well. And you dive into a story and never look back. You line up facts in a clear, orderly way. It's just that things aren't always so black and white."

I squinted at her. "Well, what else is there?"

"Shades of gray."

"I hate that!" I stood up. "I want a black-and-white world. Right and wrong. Good and bad. No questions without answers. Why can't it be like that?"

Megan shrugged. "Because people aren't like that. And because the world isn't that simple."

I felt awful. "Do you really think all those people are going to lose their jobs because of me?"

"No. They're going to lose their jobs because the company did something it shouldn't have— *if* they lose their jobs. I'm not sure they will. Tyler is angry, so he's forgetting that what went wrong with that machine can probably be fixed pretty fast if it has to be."

Megan stopped, as if something just occurred to her. "You know what else? Companies carry insurance that helps them pay government fines. Riverhead has been in this town a long time. They may have made a mistake, but they're not going to close down forever."

I picked up the letter Tyler had written. "It's going to kill me to print this. But you said it: Tyler has a right to his opinion, too."

"Maybe other kids will write in about the story," Megan said.

Glancing back at Tyler's letter, I was struck by his final line: "A voice is a powerful thing to have."

It killed me. But he was right.

Election Results Stun All!

ELECTION DAY.

The office was painfully quiet as Megan, Toni, Gary, Ringo and I sat at Dalmatian Station with empty ballots before us.

Each person wrote a name on a piece of paper and put it into the box in the center of the table.

I bit my lip, staring at my blank sheet of paper. Across from me, Megan folded her paper and put it into the box.

Taking a deep breath, I scrawled down a name, folded my paper and dropped it in.

"So . . ." Megan said nervously. "Who's going to count?"

"I have a high math aptitude," Ringo said, reaching for the box. "Especially zeros. Zeros are way cool. They're so . . . round."

I glanced away, trying not to watch as he opened the pieces of paper one by one, reading each one silently.

At last he waved the ballots in the air. "Congrats, Megan. You're the editor of *Real News*."

Megan looked totally shocked.

"You're kidding. Really? Wow, that's . . . I mean, thanks, everyone," Megan said. Her cheeks were tinged with pink as she glanced around the table.

Then her gaze landed on me, and she blinked.

"Are you going to be okay with this, Casey?" she asked. "I mean, I know how much you wanted to be editor."

Before I could answer, Ringo spoke up. "The vote was unanimous."

"What?" Megan gasped.

I hit Ringo with a rolled-up edition of *Real News*. "So much for the secret ballot!"

But Ringo was right. I *had* voted for Megan. A week ago, I'd wanted to be editor in the worst way. I could taste the ink. I knew I was the best reporter in the room. I didn't have any doubt about that. But the real question was, who was the best editor?

Megan. Definitely Megan.

I might not like it, but it was true.

Megan was eyeing me curiously now. "Thanks, Casey," she said. "That means a lot to me."

"You're not going to ask for a group hug or anything?" Gary asked hesitantly.

"Well . . ." Megan grinned at me.

"No way," I answered.

I stood up and went over to a PC. I tapped a few keys while I tried to get the words out. It wasn't easy. But it was necessary.

"You're organized, Megan. And dedicated. I mean, you stayed late inputting stories and formatting. You're open to *all* the stuff that should go into the paper. I don't have patience for kids who decorate the gym with paper chains, or jocks who bounce balls through hoops and run in circles—"

"Excuse me," Gary interrupted. "It's called *basketball*."

"Whatever," I said. "The point is"—I turned to Megan—"you're right for the job. Besides, this way I'll have more time to work on my investigative stories."

Gary shot me a worried glance. "No more canoe rides to restricted areas?"

"Don't press it," I told him.

Still thrilled, Megan clapped her hands together. "Shouldn't we start thinking about the next issue? The Halloween Dance is coming up."

"Now *there's* a hot story," I groaned. "Decorations! Focus on the great jack-o'-lantern debate. Is it cruel to carve out real, live pumpkins?"

"Been there, done that," Toni said.

Megan threw her arms around me and Toni and gave us a hug.

I rolled my eyes, but Megan didn't back off.

"This is going to be a fantastic year for us," Megan said cheerfully. "We've just given life to a newspaper! We make a super team. If we work together, who knows what we can do?"

Toni and I stared at her for a moment.

"In your sugarplum dreams, sister girl," Toni said. She slipped away from Megan and went back to cleaning her camera lenses.

I glanced over at Ringo, who was already lost, doodling a new cartoon. Gary was yelling something at a team on the portable TV.

Why was I the only one stuck in the group hug?

"We can do amazing things together!" Megan insisted. "I *know* we can!"

I slipped away from her enthusiastic embrace and grabbed my journal. "Megan? Get real."

My Word
by Linda Ellerbee

MY NAME IS LINDA ELLERBEE and I *am* a journalist, but I wasn't always. Once upon a time I was an eleven-year-old girl in Houston, Texas, a smart-mouthed, freckle-faced tomboy who was actually very shy and, not surprisingly, afraid to show it. My way of hiding my shyness was to get into someone's face and stay there. Humor was my weapon of choice. Being funny would protect me, I thought. Besides, making fun of someone was much easier than learning how to be a friend.

It will not surprise you that this method often backfired. For instance, I'd tell everyone how silly the school dance was—and be really funny doing so—then be hurt (and, yes, even surprised) when no one asked me to dance. Talk about your self-inflicted wounds. What I'm trying to say here, in case you haven't guessed, is that there's a lot of Casey in me. And the other way around.

One thing I had going for me at age eleven was a love of reading. I'm a writer today because I was a reader back then. My library card was a cherished thing, a ticket out of loneliness, out of feeling that I was *different*, and out of my almost total ignorance about almost everything not taught in class. Books opened that door for me—and there were no boundaries, not even time. When I was eleven, girls were supposed to be frilly, silly little pieces of fluff who thought acting empty-headed around boys was smart. But I could read *Little Women*, which took place in the 1860s, and meet a girl who intended to grow up and *do* things—to travel, have adventures, write stories. Like Casey (and like me), Jo March cared about the world outside her own life. Jo read books and newspapers; she had opinions about slavery, the Civil War, the roles of men and women—and she wasn't afraid to speak up, to act, to try to change her world. Or I could read a Nancy Drew mystery and get to know still another girl who was fearless, who set out to find answers to her questions and wasn't very good with the word "no." I liked girls like Jo and Nancy. I needed them.

Today we see strong women all around us, but that's not enough, because it's *still* hard to be a girl. (It just *is*, that's why.) So it's still necessary for girls to be able to know other girls who are brave and daring and very, very real—even when they're made up. I know Casey has a lot of flaws— she's insecure and can be desperately annoying, and her mouth regularly gets her in large trouble, but she dreams big and she's not afraid to try to make her dreams come true. I want that for *all* girls. (Yes, of course I want it for boys, *too*. What did you think?)

And I like it when kids care about that bigger world. I'm executive producer and host of a television series called *Nick News*. It's a news and documentary series for kids. You may have seen it on Nickelodeon. On our programs, we show how the distant and global affect you, and how you can affect the distant and global. We assume you're smart people; we don't talk down to you. We just try to tell you what happened. So you can see what you think.

As Casey says, news isn't hard. Mostly it's the answer to the question: "What happened?" The rest is storytelling. And journalism—as I would grow up to discover—is a pretty good way for a shy person to see the world and get to know some of its most fascinating people. I guess you could say that instead of learning how to keep my mouth shut, I learned how to keep it open and get paid for doing so. (Somewhere along the way, I think I also learned how to be a friend.)

However, although Casey and I share a lot of characteristics, I didn't have Casey's passion for journalism when I was eleven. Sure, I read the newspaper every day—okay, mostly the comics, sports page and my horoscope (I'm a Leo)—but at that time I still wanted to grow up to play third base for the New York Yankees. When they told me you had to be a guy, I got so steamed I decided to become a cocker spaniel, instead. All right, I outgrew wanting to bite people on the ankles—but I never outgrew my love of reading and telling stories, which led me, later on, to become a journalist, and then, much later on, to tell you stories about Casey and Megan and Gary and Toni and—probably my fave—Ringo. What I mean to do here is to tell stories about kids, especially girls, who think for themselves, who aren't perfect, or even likeable all the time, and who always live in—*and are passionate about*—a world where there might be more than one answer to a question.

Call it the real world.

I know this much about *you*. You already live in that world. And you know it. So you *go*. Change it. Shape it. Own it. Get going. Get real.